DOCTOR · WHO

ANNUAL 2006

EDITOR **CLAYTON HICKMAN**
DESIGNER **PERI GODBOLD**

FRONTISPIECE ILLUSTRATION BY **ALISTER PEARSON**
PUZZLES BY **JUSTIN RICHARDS** & **GARETH ROBERTS**
PUZZLE PAGE ILLUSTRATIONS BY **BEN MORRIS**

WITH THANKS TO **RUSSELL T DAVIES, TOM SPILSBURY, JAMES CLARKSON, IAN GRUTCHFIELD, FRANCINE HOLDGATE, NICK PEGG, JAMES HAWES, KATE BEHARRELL, RICHARD HOLLIS** & **ROSEMARIE HARRISON.**

PANINI BOOKS

£6.99

D0246789

Who's Who?

WRITTEN BY **PHILIP MACDONALD**

The universe is a magical place. Ancient, mysterious and unimaginably vast, it seems to us as we gaze upwards from our little planet to be both dark and silent.

And yet whirling through its inky blackness are a million trillion burning stars, around which spin countless strange worlds, crackling with light, sound, colour and life.

Out there among the stars mighty civilisations rise and fall, leaving monuments to their glory in the form of great cities, great discoveries, great legacies of peace and prosperity.

But it is also a place of darkness and of danger: in some corners of the universe dwell creatures who are driven not by a love of life, but by a burning desire to conquer and destroy all that comes in their way. There are the Nestenes, a race of ruthless invaders with the power to breathe life into anything made of plastic; there are the Sontarans, vicious goblin-like warriors locked in an unending intergalactic conflict with the gelatinous Rutans; the Gelth, a ghostly gaseous life-force vampirically seeking out bodies to inhabit; the grotesque shape-shifting Zygons, intent on colonising Earth; the Slitheen, a deadly criminal clan from the planet Raxacoricofallapatorius; the mighty Cybermen, who were once human beings themselves before they began replacing their bodily organs with robotic components, and who now patrol the universe in search of bodies to convert into their own ghoulish kind; the terrifying Reapers, voracious scavengers of the time vortex; and most terrible of all, the dreaded Daleks, mutated monsters from the planet Skaro who long ago retreated into lethal armoured war-machines, their twisted minds genetically engineered to despise all other life in the cosmos.

Throughout the boundless tracts of space and time, creatures both good and evil roam the galaxies, sometimes laying waste to entire planets in their thirst for conquest, and sometimes merely interrupting the affairs of an innocent bystander or two when they touch down unexpectedly on a world that has yet to develop interplanetary travel. A world such as Earth, for example...

ENTER ROSE...

When London teenager Rose Tyler found herself in the midst of an attempted invasion by the Nestenes and their plastic servants the Autons, it was the beginning of an adventure that no human being could begin to dream of. Luckily for Rose, and luckily for our planet too, the Nestenes were not the only alien life-form visiting London that day. There was someone else in town: a lonely, mysterious wanderer known only as the Doctor. But Rose was soon to discover, that the Doctor is no ordinary traveller. For one thing, his voyages are by no means restricted to the present day; his ship, the TARDIS, can travel through time as well as space. He can just as easily pop back to the 19th Century to visit Charles Dickens as touch down on a giant space station in the distant future.

So who is this mysterious, mercurial man? Where do he and his amazing space-time machine come from? As Rose gets to know him a little better, she begins to discover that there's more to the Doctor than meets the eye...

Despite his youthful appearance, the Doctor is far older than any human; at the last count he was reckoned to be around 900 years old. He belongs to an ancient and powerful race called the Time Lords, but he long ago turned his back on their sedate, monastic lifestyle on the distant planet of Gallifrey and decided instead to explore the universe. To that end the Doctor 'borrowed' the TARDIS – a marvel of Time Lord technology whose name stands for 'Time And Relative Dimension In Space' – and set off on his travels, never intending to return.

Like all Time Lords, the Doctor is blessed with remarkable qualities. He has two hearts and an unusually powerful cardio-vascular system, and he even has the ability to 'regenerate' his body if it is injured or threatened at times of great crisis. When a regeneration occurs, the Doctor's appearance undergoes a complete transformation, and although the man within remains the same, his outward behaviour and habits are drastically altered. This has happened several times already: in fact, the Doctor who befriended Rose during the Nestene invasion was the ninth incarnation of the wandering Time Lord. And Rose has only just witnessed the miracle of regeneration first-hand...

THE CHANGING FACE OF DOCTOR WHO

The original Doctor, who stole the TARDIS from his people and set off on his travels many centuries ago, appeared at first sight to be very different from the heroic figure that Rose has come to know and trust. He looked and behaved like an elderly, white-haired English gentleman, rather old-fashioned in his ways and in his sartorial tastes; he wouldn't have looked out of place in the England of Queen Victoria or Edward VII. We first encountered him back in 1963, when two London schoolteachers called Ian and Barbara decided to follow a mysterious pupil, Susan, back to her home to discuss her schoolwork with her grandfather. They discovered to their astonishment that

Susan's home address was nothing more than an old junkyard, in which stood a police telephone box – a familiar feature of the British landscape in the 1960s, long before the days of walkie-talkies and mobile phones. But this was no ordinary police box. Beyond its doors, Ian and Barbara found an impossibly huge alien control room, and learned that both Susan and her grandfather – the Doctor himself – were exiles from another race. Fearing discovery, the old Doctor activated the controls, whisking Susan, Ian and Barbara off on a series of thrilling adventures in time and space – including the first ever encounter with the Daleks.

It soon became apparent that the Doctor enjoyed only limited control over the TARDIS, and could not always predict with any accuracy where – or, for that matter, when – the ship would materialise next. Another problem was the breakdown of the chameleon circuit, an alien device which allows the exterior shape of a fully functional TARDIS to blend in with its surroundings wherever it lands: while the cavernous interior remains the same, the outward appearance of the ship might become a rock, or a tree, or a statue. But the Doctor's TARDIS is faulty, meaning that the ship remains stuck in the form of a police box: perfect for blending into the background in 1960s London, but rather incongruous at any other location in time and space.

The original Doctor could sometimes be cantankerous and ill-tempered, but he also had a lovable, cuddly side and a keen sense of humour; and whatever his mood, his great wisdom always shone through. He travelled in the TARDIS for three years, bidding farewell to his original companions and making new friends along the way. During his first encounter with the terrible Cybermen, the Doctor declared that his old body was 'wearing a bit thin', and later unexpectedly collapsed in the

TOP: The Ninth Doctor at the controls of his ship. ABOVE: Our first-ever look at the TARDIS – stuck in a junkyard in 1960s London. RIGHT: The First Doctor was grumpy and irritable, but also loveable and kind-hearted. INSET: The terrible Cybermen invade the South Pole.

6

FAR LEFT: The Second Doctor cut a comedic figure. **INSET:** The TARDIS lands in the Himalayas and its crew face the Abominable Snowmen! **BELOW:** The dashing Third Doctor was an Earthbound man of action – facing fearsome foes such as the aquatic Sea Devils, the malevolent Master, and of course the deadly Daleks!

EXILED TO EARTH!

And so the Third Doctor arrived on the scene: a tall, strikingly elegant, grey-haired patrician with a taste for the finer things in life – good wines, velvet jackets and embroidered shirts, and a newfound flair for a form of unarmed combat called Venusian Aikido. Confined to 20th-Century Earth, his TARDIS disabled by the Time Lords, the Third Doctor spent much of his time working for a military organisation called UNIT, helping to repel alien invasions (including the first two assaults on Earth by the Nestenes) and terrestrial menaces such as a plague of giant maggots created by industrial pollution, and the revival of a prehistoric reptile race called the Silurians who had gone into hibernation many millions of years before mankind evolved.

TARDIS control room. Before the astonished eyes of his friends, the Doctor's body began to change, his features dissolving into those of a younger, dark-haired man. The Second Doctor had arrived: a rumpled, unlidy little fellow with an impish twinkle in his eye and a constant sense of fun, shot through with the penetrating intelligence that always burns beneath the Doctor's outward appearance.

During his second incarnation, the Doctor encountered a host of new foes including the reptilian Ice Warriors, the robotic Yeti and the crab-like Macra, as well as battling the Daleks and the Cybermen on many occasions. He was also the first Doctor to make use of the sonic screwdriver, an indispensable gadget that can tackle anything from opening electronic locks to detonating explosives. The Second Doctor's days came to an end when he found himself up against a force so powerful that he had no choice but to seek assistance from his own people; and so, six years into his travels, television viewers finally learned the truth about the Doctor's origins. For the first time the omnipotent Time Lords appeared, overthrowing the terrible evil of the alien War Games and promptly capturing the Doctor, who had absconded from their planet so long ago. Put on trial by his own people for interfering in the ways of other worlds, the Doctor argued that his particular kind of interference was sometimes necessary: to stand by and observe is not always enough, because there is evil in the universe that must be fought. The Time Lords accepted the Doctor's argument, and reduced his sentence to exile on the planet Earth in a newly regenerated body.

afterwards, the Third Doctor met his final challenge in the form of the giant spiders of Metebelis III, whose cave of psychoactive crystals irradiated his body beyond recovery; collapsing to the floor at UNIT headquarters, the Doctor once again changed his appearance.

NEW DOCTORS, OLD ENEMIES

With his manic eyes, halo of curly hair and jumbled wardrobe of frock coat, tweed trousers and an absurdly long scarf, the Fourth Doctor was an elemental force of nature, a wildly eccentric adventurer who wasted no time in severing his ties with UNIT and setting off once again to explore the cosmos at large. He threw himself into each new adventure with an air of wide-eyed wonder, greeting friends and foes alike with a toothy smile and a crumpled bag of jelly babies. He did battle with the Daleks, Cybermen and Sontarans, and also crossed paths with many fearful new adversaries including the wasp-like Wirrn, the giant Krynoids, the stone Ogri, the one-eyed Jagaroth, a swarm of space vampires, an ancient death-force called the Fendahl, and the supreme malevolence of a god-like being called Sutekh. But it was a familiar foe who finally defeated the fourth Doctor: the Master, too, had regenerated into a new body, and it was during an epic confrontation with his arch-enemy that the Doctor fell from the gantry of a radio-telescope, and was forced to regenerate his shattered form.

The Silurians' marine cousins, the Sea Devils, also menaced the Third Doctor, as did a host of other foes including the Axons, the Sontarans, the Ogrons and of course the ever-present Daleks. But the Third Doctor's most persistent enemy was one of his own people, a rogue Time Lord known as the Master: long ago on Gallifrey the two had been boyhood friends, but now the Master's ambitions had turned towards domination and conquest. He would stop at nothing to achieve his nefarious aims, even joining forces with aliens like the Nestenes and the Daleks when it served his purposes.

The Time Lords eventually restored the Third Doctor's freedom to roam in time and space as a reward for defeating the gravest peril their people had ever faced: in fact, so extraordinary was this particular adventure that the Doctor found himself crossing his own time-stream and joining forces with his two previous selves to defeat the megalomaniac Omega. Not long

The Fifth Doctor was a younger, more straightforwardly heroic figure, with a fresh face, flowing blond hair and a penchant for the quintessentially English pastime of cricket. His optimistic, often headstrong nature led him into many a tight spot, once again pitting his wits against Daleks, Cybermen, Sea Devils and the Master, as well as a parade of new monsters like the

TOP: Military organisation UNIT often helped the Doctor defeat alien invasions. **LEFT:** The Fourth Doctor was a fun-loving force of nature. **INSET:** One of the warlike Sontarans. **BELOW LEFT:** A Time Lord – one of the Doctor's own people – in ceremonial robes. **BELOW RIGHT:** Davros, evil creator of the Daleks.

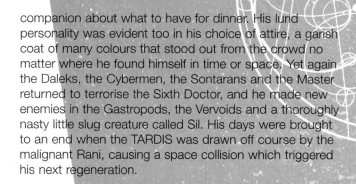

companion about what to have for dinner. His lurid personality was evident too in his choice of attire, a garish coat of many colours that stood out from the crowd no matter where he found himself in time or space. Yet again the Daleks, the Cybermen, the Sontarans and the Master returned to terrorise the Sixth Doctor, and he made new enemies in the Gastropods, the Vervoids and a thoroughly nasty little slug creature called Sil. His days were brought to an end when the TARDIS was drawn off course by the malignant Rani, causing a space collision which triggered his next regeneration.

REGENERATION GAMES

And so to Doctor number seven, a mystical, elfin figure with a dishevelled charm and a quiet authority. This Doctor was much given to quiet contemplation and mysterious brooding, approaching his battles as though he were playing a game of chess with the forces of darkness. And sure enough, the forces of darkness were ranged against him: in addition to the Daleks, Cybermen and the Master, the Seventh Doctor found himself confronting such memorable foes as the blood-sucking Haemovores, the demonic Destroyer and the baleful Gods of Ragnarok. He met his final showdown in a hail of bullets on the streets of San Francisco, when the TARDIS materialised amid an outbreak of gang warfare. The Doctor was rushed to a nearby hospital and declared dead by the unsuspecting medics… until he regenerated and rose from his slab to the terror of a mortuary attendant, who happened to be watching an old Frankenstein movie at the time!

The Eighth Doctor's adventures barely lasted long enough for us to get to

amphibious Terileptils, the devilish Malus, the gravity-controlling Tractators and the psychic terrors of the Mara, which invaded his companion's mind and manifested itself as a giant snake. In the end it was the Fifth Doctor's reckless heroism that led to his downfall: on the planet Androzani Minor both he and his companion Peri became poisoned by a deadly substance called spectrox, and the Doctor's desperate struggle to find the antidote in time to save Peri meant that there was no time to save himself; and so he had no choice but to regenerate once again.

If the Fifth Doctor had been a polite, companionable sort of fellow, his successor presented an immediate contrast: the Sixth Doctor was brash, tactless and enjoyed nothing more than a blazing quarrel, whether it was with a fearsome alien tyrant about the future of the universe, or with his hapless

TOP: The fresh-faced Fifth Doctor. **LEFT:** The Sixth Doctor had a unique taste in clothes!. **RIGHT:** The mysterious and manipulative Seventh Doctor. **INSET TOP:** The twisted Sharaz-Jek helped end the Doctor's fifth life. **INSET ABOVE:** Two wicked Time Lords – the Master and the Rani.

know him, consisting of a single TV movie in which he battled the ever-resourceful Master while getting to grips with his new body. Like several of his earlier incarnations, the Eighth Doctor cut a Byronic figure with long flowing hair and a taste for Victorian apparel. We last saw him in 1996, whereafter *Doctor Who* vanished from our screens… until now.

NINTH TIME LUCKY?

The Ninth Doctor embodies all of the Time Lord's legendary qualities, and yet, just like his predecessors, he brings to the character a new twist and a style that is all his own. He has the same universal wisdom, the same encyclopaedic knowledge of the universe, and the same unwavering sense of morality; and yet despite all this, he is perhaps the least other-worldly, most down-to-earth Time Lord of them all. Gone are the flowing hair and the antique frock-coats, cravats and tweeds so often favoured by his predecessors; instead, the Ninth Doctor is at home in a leather jacket, T-shirt and jeans. But he has lost none of his natural authority: his is still a commanding presence, striding into unfamiliar surroundings and effortlessly taking control of

situations when the need arises. He is still possessed of an innocent, infectious vigour, a wide-eyed sense of adventure and wonder, a child-like quality that has never deserted him since the day he chose to set off and see the wonders of the universe.

But this Doctor carries a dreadful burden that none of his predecessors could have imagined. He has seen his whole world destroyed – ravaged by a terrible Time War with the Daleks – and the Doctor is the only one of his people to have survived the carnage. He is the last of the Time Lords, alone in the universe...

Perhaps because of this, he has a keen, almost rapturous appreciation for everything that is beautiful in the cosmos. He finds joy and wonder in the very movement of the stars and planets. He is driven by an indefatigable love of life, and he is eager to share all of this with his friends.

And this is one of the things that make the Doctor unique. Unlike most adventure heroes, the Doctor does not have a job. He isn't a policeman, or a detective, or a Time Agent. He doesn't get summoned to the scene of the crime. He doesn't work for anybody. He is a free spirit: a traveller, an explorer, a sightseer. He's in it for the ride. He is a living, breathing embodiment of the adventurer in us all, and we admire him because he has done the very thing that we all wish we could do from time to time: he has cut the chains of a conventional life and spread his wings out into the universe.

But the Doctor is not an irresponsible traveller. He is not a meddler, and he doesn't go looking for trouble: in fact, the only thing that compels him to pit his wits against the forces of evil is his own keen sense of what is right and what is wrong. He deplores violence, and will always strive to find peaceful solutions to conflict, but on those occasions when he encounters injustice or tyranny, he finds it impossible to look the other way. Despite his powers of regeneration the Doctor is just as fragile and mortal as the rest of us – not even his Time Lord abilities would save him from a Dalek's gun or the ravages of the time vortex – and yet he has the courage to place himself in terrible danger when the universe is in peril.

In fact, to put it simply, the Doctor is a hero. And the universe will always need one of those. ●

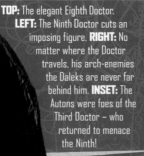

TOP: The elegant Eighth Doctor. **LEFT:** The Ninth Doctor cuts an imposing figure. **RIGHT:** No matter where the Doctor travels, his arch-enemies the Daleks are never far behind him. **INSET:** The Autons were foes of the Third Doctor – who returned to menace the Ninth!

ROBOT·ROSE!

The mischievous, meddlesome Breebles hatched a plan to take their revenge on the Doctor after he destroyed their replication pods. They created an almost perfect robotic duplicate of Rose Tyler – and kidnapped the real Rose!

The robot took her place, with orders to kill the Doctor! But the real Rose escaped from the Breebles and rejoined the Doctor – leaving him with a big dilemma.

Which Rose was real – and which one was the killer robot?

To find the answer, the Doctor asked both Rose Tylers to give an account of their past adventures. The real Rose, of course, answered correctly, but the robot Rose – whose memory disk had been inaccurately copied – made ten mistakes.

The Doctor spotted the mistakes and deactivated the killer robot with his sonic screwdriver. But could you spot the ten mix-ups that gave the electronic impostor away?

"It all started when I got attacked by walking shop window dummies – plastic brought to life by the Slitheen. I left behind my mum and my boyfriend Mike and joined you in the TARDIS.

Our first stop was to see the end of the world, in the year two billion – then we went back in time to Edinburgh in 1869 and met Charles Dickens, who helped us defeat the Gelth. After that you took me back home, only to find the Nestenes trying to blow up the world by disguising themselves as journalists.

In the year 2012 we landed in Canada and I accidentally freed the last Dalek – after you killed it, we took Adam on board; then we travelled to the space station Satellite 9, where we met the evil Cassandra."

Check your answers against the Doctor's list of Robot Rose's mix-ups on page 62!

TARDIS TEASER

The Daleks have found the TARDIS. But the dematerialisation circuit is not working, and the Doctor is busy trying to fix it. Captain Jack needs to work out which Dalek ships are least dangerous so he can plot an escape route using the TARDIS's spacedrive..

See if you can work out the answer to the question he puts to the TARDIS computers, then compare your answer with the one the TARDIS gave on page 62:

"We have been discovered by ten Dalek ships. From their sensor profiles, we know that three have ruby ray lasers, six have atomic cannons, and two have both. How many of the Dalek ships are unarmed?"

WRITTEN BY
GARETH ROBERTS

ILLUSTRATIONS BY
ANDY WALKER

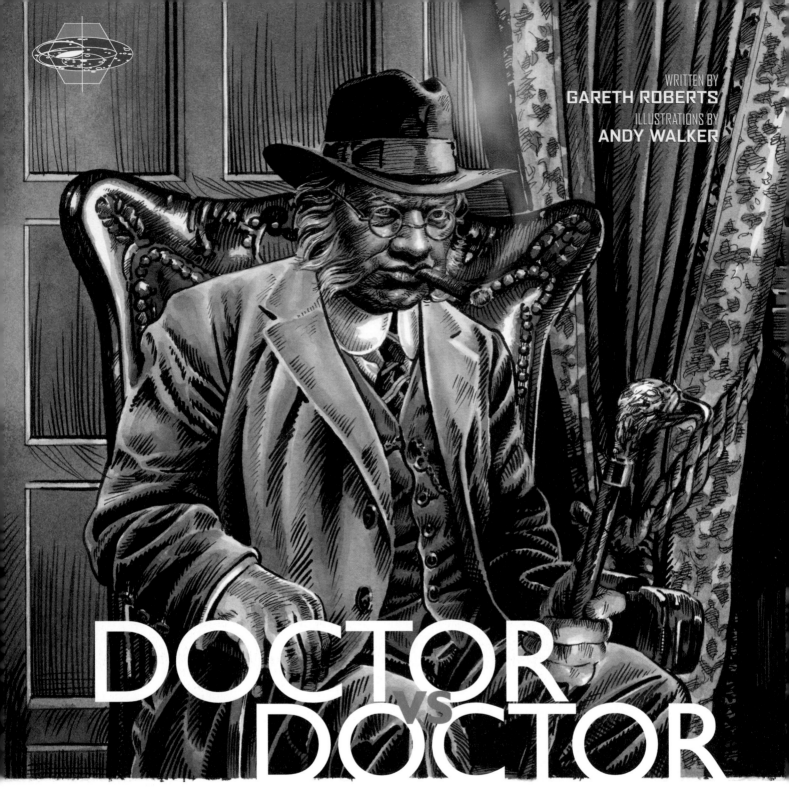

DOCTOR vs DOCTOR

OCTOR MERRIVALE CARR SAT SILENTLY
in the corner of the library, blinking owlishly
behind the thick glass of his spectacles, his
enormous waistcoated frame barely contained
in the studded leather armchair, his eagle-
topped cane clutched in one pudgy hand, a huge cigar
clamped in his mouth, his prodigious whiskers and broken-
veined face shadowed by the brim of his extraordinary hat.

As always his young American friend, Henry Ransom,
could barely credit the doctor's almost laughably bluff
exterior with containing the sharp intelligence and genius
for deduction that had solved some of the most baffling
mysteries in the history of crime. The Case of the Gilded
Mouse; The Matter of the Laughing Bicyclist; The Problem
Of the Bitten Wire – each had seemed impenetrable to
the finest minds of Scotland Yard, and each had been
unravelled by the doctor's incredible, if unorthodox, mind.
Ransom had written up the cases in a series of best-selling

volumes, making Dr Carr famous internationally. And
now, at the climax of recent events at the country retreat of
Lord Farthingale (in which first the Lord's prospective son-
in-law Sebastian Marten had been inexplicably battered to
death in the locked billiard room, and then his accountant
Paul Steiffers had been impaled on an antique Turkish
sword in his locked bedroom, with not one footprint in the
snow outside the open window) it seemed as if Dr Carr
was about to carve yet another notch on his post. Ransom
felt sure he would soon have another book to write.

Dr Carr had asked Lord Farthingale and his house guests
– his remaining house guests – to assemble in the library
where he would finally explain all. The fierce winter wind
roared along the valley outside, yet inside this crowded
room all was silent but for the crackling of logs in the fire
and the sonorous ticking of the grandfather clock. Ransom
took another look at the people caught up in the bizarre
events; Lord Farthingale himself, stiff-backed and querulous

with his shock of white hair; his beautiful daughter Janet, whose perfect jaw was tightened with tension; Stephen Carter, the Lord's secretary, thin-lipped and weak-chinned; Bart Faversham, the deceased Sebastian Marten's best friend, rugged and healthy in his sports coat; and Glenda Neil, the dark-eyed society hostess, whose legendary beauty had started to dim in middle age. All their eyes were turned to Dr Carr.

Dr Carr gave a harrumph – unnecessary, as he already held their attention. 'Thank you for gathering here,' he wheezed. 'First off, let me admit something. I've been a fool. A damned fool. If I had noticed a vital clue earlier than I did, Steiffers need not have died. I could have run down our murderer two nights ago, after Sebastian's death. But I overlooked something – something tiny, but in plain sight.' He coughed. 'Something the murderer – let us call him or her X – had overlooked also.'

Bart Faversham groaned. 'For heaven's sake, old man,' he protested. 'Do we have to go through all this blether? Do you know who did it?'

'Oh yes,' said Dr Carr, fixing him with an oddly penetrating look. 'I have known X's identity for some hours now. And X is sitting here... *in this very room!*'

He shifted his massive bulk a little forward in his chair. 'Let us go back to the night of Sebastian's murder. Lord Farthingale has told us how he was the last to retire, at a quarter past midnight, having made his customary nightly inspection of all the window and door locks of the house. Sebastian had quarrelled with Mr Faversham in the trophy room an hour earlier –'

'Look here, Dr Carr,' said Bart. 'Seb and I argued all the time, there was nothing peculiar about –'

Dr Carr raised one of his paddle-like hands. 'Thank you, I am aware of that. I am simply putting together a picture of the last few hours Sebastian Marten spent on Earth. As I say, exasperated by the quarrel, Sebastian had retired to his bed in the east wing, Mr Faversham to his in the west wing. At around one in the morning, Mrs New, m'lord's admirable cook, has told us she heard somebody moving about – stealthily – in the corridor beyond the servants' quarters, which of course leads to the billiard room. She looked through the door and saw the silhouette of a man. That, she has sworn, was Sebastian Marten. A few minutes later, Mrs New swears she heard the door of the billiard room open and close. And of course in the morning he was found there, almost every bone in his body broken in a brutal attack. And yet – the door of the billiard room was supposedly locked, and Lord Farthingale had the key in his possession all night, as witnessed by Mr Carter.'

'We know all this,' sighed Glenda Neil.

'Now – we concentrated very much on the *how* of Sebastian's death. Not enough on the *why*. Sebastian was a promising young journalist at the *Sunday Clarion*, with an incredible facility for recall – and a remarkable memory for faces.' He turned to Janet. 'Remember what you said about him? "Sebastian never forgets a face."'

Janet nodded nervously, and Bart Faversham patted her supportively on the shoulder. Ransom quivered inside. For he loved Janet Farthingale – with a purity and a respect for her academic mind that neither her dead cad of a fiancée or Faversham could ever muster.

Dr Carr went on. 'And therein lies the clue to the case. Sebastian never forgot a face. And that face belonged to Kitty Kickshaw.'

Lord Farthingale spluttered. 'Who is Kitty Kickshaw?'

'Strictly speaking, nobody,' said Dr Carr. 'Kitty Kickshaw was the stage name of a Broadway entertainer of twenty years ago. A male impersonator. And someone

whose name Sebastian 'accidentally' dropped before all of us earlier that very night. You see, Sebastian identified her face – although twenty years on from the archive photograph he had seen – as somebody in this house. And with his gambling debts, he saw a way to blackmail her.'

Glenda Neil sprung from her chair. 'This is preposterous!'

'Yes, it would have meant ruin – for *you*,' said Dr Carr. 'For the world to discover that Glenda Neil, famed English society hostess, was in reality nothing but a hoofer from Dixie. And you were prepared to kill to protect that secret. You arranged to meet Sebastian Marten in the billiard room that night – it was you who Mrs New saw padding about, using your long-disused male impersonation skills. And it was you who palmed the key to the billiard room from Lord Farthingale.'

Glena Neil's eyes widened. 'But this simply isn't true!' She turned pleadingly to Carter. 'Stephen, this man is talking nonsense!'

'Poor Steiffers deduced the truth,' Dr Carr continued inexorably. 'He realised you, Mrs Neil, were the only possible candidate for the past of Kitty Kickshaw. So he became the next victim. Using an elaborate system of weights and pulleys from the stables, you opened the window of Steiffers' bedroom from the window above. Then you slipped down on a rope, and knocked Steiffers to his death with a broom handle – and he fell back on to the scimitar you had placed upright at his bedside.' Dr Carr shook his head and emitted a massive wheeze. 'Reputation … you were prepared to kill for it, twice.'

Ransom was expecting Glenda Neil to capitulate – but then, something extraordinary happened. The library door burst open and the strangest people he had ever seen entered the room.

The first was a man of indeterminate age, dressed in the rough leather clothes of some kind of labourer. His features were uneven, with bright blue eyes that flashed with an almost dangerous intensity. He wore an expression of amusement and, oddly for a working man, carried himself with self-assurance and authority. His companion was the strangest – and, Ransom thought, possibly the most beautiful – young woman he had ever seen. She wore the clothing of a boy; bizarre canvas trousers, and a kind of hooded jerkin with no buttons, and her long fair hair framed a face that combined the typical vigour of a servant girl with an astonishingly relaxed sensuality.

'Sorry, mate,' said the man casually to Dr Carr. 'Been listening at the door. Bad habit, I know... Good try, except you've only got it *totally* wrong.'

FOR ROSE, IT HAD STARTED ABOUT AN HOUR before, inside the TARDIS. She'd entered the control room to find the Doctor with his head under the console and one long arm stretched up and tapping at the computer keyboard. There was a worrying grinding noise coming from somewhere deep inside the TARDIS's workings.

Rose leaned over the Doctor's shoulder for a closer look. He was tapping at a tiny component with a tool that looked like a wrench but probably wasn't. 'Technical stuff?' she asked.

'Technical problem, actually,' grunted the Doctor. Rose saw that he had some rusty screws in his mouth. She put out her hand, and the Doctor spat them into her palm with a nod of thanks and one of his sudden, devastating smiles. 'Nothing I can't sort,' he continued, tapping at the

keyboard again. He nodded to the police box doors. 'There's something out there...'

Rose checked the central column, which was moving up and down. 'Hang on, but we haven't landed yet. There's nothing out there.'

The Doctor shrugged. 'Do you fancy a really, really complicated explanation?'

'Could you manage just a bit complicated?'

'I'll give it a go.' The Doctor stood up, rattled at the space bar on the keyboard, and frowned. 'We're in the vortex, right? Well, somebody at the corresponding co-ordinates in real time is running a –' He paused.

'Just a bit complicated,' reminded Rose.

'– an engine,' went on the Doctor, 'that's affecting ours.'

'I got that,' said Rose, smiling. 'See, you can do it.'

The Doctor rattled at the space bar again. 'Thought I could over-ride the quantum interference from here, but the computer won't let me. I could work out the code to get round it, but that'd take a day or two, I'm useless in DOS...' He flipped over a familiar set of levers, leaping from panel to panel of the console.

'So instead we're going to materialise and ask them to turn it off,' said Rose.

'Only for a second,' said the Doctor, 'then them and us can be on our merry way. I'll just check where we're gonna come out...' He squinted at a glowing panel and his face fell. 'Oh great, yeah, it'd have to be there. It'd have to be then, and there.'

He moved away from the panel and Rose took his place reading off the dial. 'Earth, 1920. Where nobody should be running that kind of – engine. So this isn't just gonna be "Hi, let's swap insurance details"?'

'Nope. It's probably gonna be deadly danger and aliens without a good enough reason to be there.'

Rose's face lit up with delight. 'Got any 20s clothes back there? I wanna do the whole "Modern Millie" thing …'

'No time,' said the Doctor, slipping into his jacket. 'We've gotta fix this quick. Plus I look a right git in Oxford bags.'

The sound of ancient engines, groaning in protest even more than they usually did, started to shake the TARDIS as it materialised.

WHO IN HEAVEN'S NAME ARE YOU, SIR?' demanded Lord Farthingale. 'And how did you enter this house?'

The newcomer looked amused, as if he'd heard the question a million times before and was trying to think of a new way to answer it. 'I'm the Doctor. And I'm parked upstairs.' He smiled at the girl. 'It makes a change, tell the truth once in a while.' He gestured to her. 'This is my best friend Rose.'

The manners, appearance and words of these two extraordinary visitors was almost too much for Ransom to take in. He looked instinctively at Dr Carr for his reaction. The old man had risen from his chair, and supporting his mighty bulk on his stick he tottered over to the strangers. 'I don't care who or what you are,' he said confidently. 'But I care very much about your impertinence. By Cicero's beard! What leads you to question my deductions?'

'Could you take that cheroot out of my face, ta?' asked the man who called himself the Doctor, coughing a little. He slapped his hands together. 'Right everybody. If you want to stay alive, get out of this house.'

Bart Faversham stepped forward. 'Are you threatening us?' He slipped a protective arm round Janet Farthingale, who looked as stunned as everyone else, making Ransom quiver inside with envy.

'Nope, I'm saving your lives,' said the Doctor plainly.

'I ask you again!' thundered Dr Carr, puffing a very deliberate cloud into the Doctor's face. 'What's your beef with my conclusions?'

The girl Rose answered. 'It's all a lot simpler than you think. In one way. And much, much more complicated in another way. And he's right about getting out of here.'

'Or you can stay and definitely die,' said the Doctor. 'Your choice.' He made to leave the way he had come, but Dr Carr, with a speed and vigour surprising even to an acquaintance of such long standing as Ransom, expertly blocked his path.

'I demand an explanation,' he spluttered.

'Look,' said the Doctor, 'you're probably right about everything normally, but just this once you're out of your depth. Don't worry, we won't tell anyone.'

Dr Carr pointed to Glenda Neil. 'This woman murdered

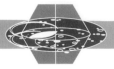

Sebastian Marten and Steiffers!'

'No,' said Rose. 'Invisible aliens murdered them. The Doctor worked it out while we were listening in.' The Doctor shot her a look that was half reproving, half affectionate, and she shrugged. 'Makes a change to tell the truth...'

'Invisible aliens?' coughed Dr Carr, relaxing visibly. 'You know, for a moment there I thought you possibly had a serious objection to my methods and results. Now you've proved yourself to be simply insane.'

The Doctor seemed to come to a decision. He looked Dr Carr straight in the eye with a penetrating stare. 'Methods and results... okay. Are you the kind of person who reckons he can tell everything about someone just by looking at 'em? Where he's from, the name of his tailor, his job, who he's married to, all that?'

Ransom spoke up for the first time. 'That's certainly true. Dr Carr makes a very quick study of any stranger.'

The Doctor spread his arms wide, as if putting himself

on display before Dr Carr. 'Go on then.'

Dr Carr hesitated, his mouth opening and closing silently, his eyes flicking up and down the strange Doctor. At several moments he looked as if he was about to say something, to pull some incredible revelation out of the hat, but finally he merely shook his head and grumbled into his whiskers.

The Doctor grabbed the girl Rose, rather uncouthly although she didn't seem to mind at all, and placed her in front of Dr Carr. 'How about Rose, then?'

Rose smiled a little awkwardly – and her appearance had the same effect on Dr Carr. 'Sorry,' she said, stepping back.

'See?' said the Doctor. 'Don't be too hard on yourself.'

'Yeah, hardly anyone can work him out,' put in Rose.

Dr Carr huffed. 'Nothing makes sense, nothing fits,' he mumbled. He gestured to the Doctor. 'Your accent doesn't match your manners, your clothes don't match your face, your watch is set to completely the wrong time, and your shoes are... most peculiar.'

'Rose's are worse,' said the Doctor. Ransom looked down and saw that the girl was wearing a pair of something like padded track shoes. 'Now, I really mean it about getting out of here,' the Doctor continued. 'I'm not just using my mouth for the sake of it.'

Bart Faversham, who had spent the last few incredible moments in a stunned torpor shared by nearly all the inhabitants of the room, suddenly leapt up. 'Damned lunatics, the pair of you!' he shouted. '"Invisible aliens?" It wouldn't surprise me if you had done away with Seb and old Steiffers, and now you're planning more of the same for us! I suggest we phone the local station and –'

Suddenly Janet screamed – a long high-pitched piercing note.

For Ransom, the next half a second was utter confusion. A peculiar buzzing sound seemed to come from everywhere at once. His view of the room seemed to swim, as if a heat haze had sprung up from nowhere. And Bart Faversham was bodily lifted into the air by something that simply wasn't there.

It was as if a giant invisible hand had grabbed the young

man's strong, lithe frame. He dangled for a moment before them, his eyes bulging in uncomprehending terror, and then suddenly he was flung across the room with a whoosh of compressed air – and straight into the fire. Ransom winced at the ghastly crack of Faversham's head on the hearth. The buzzing sound stopped as if it had been flicked off by a switch, and the weird swimming of the air subsided at the same moment. There was another half a second of silence – and then, the women (except Rose) screaming and the men cursing, everybody ran from the room through the door which the Doctor was holding open obligingly, for all the world like a commissionaire on duty outside a Park Lane hotel.

'Come on!' the Doctor shouted at the frozen Ransom.

Ransom jerked into life, tumbling through the door.

'OH YEAH, EVERYONE BELIEVES ME WHEN IT'S too late!' exclaimed the Doctor, at the head of the small terrified group, a few seconds later, as he threw open the front doors of the house. Ransom gulped. The air around the house was thrumming with what could only be electricity. The Doctor slammed the doors shut and leant back against them.

'So it's all around us,' said Rose.

'Yeah, they're trying to engage their drive again,' said the Doctor. 'Only safe place'll be the TARDIS... Right, everyone upstairs!' He pointed to the stairway, and such was the authority in his tone that Ransom, along with all the others, dashed to obey.

But the stairway was contaminated by the same ghastly swimming haze they had seen in the library!

Rose threw open the nearest door, which led to the billiard room. 'In here!' she cried, and they set off again, piling through almost on top of one another, Dr Carr bringing up the rear, puffing and limping along. To his indignation, the Doctor virtually picked him up and carried him the last few steps of the way.

In the billiard room there was no sign of any of the strange disturbances that had afflicted the rest of the house and killed Faversham. Ransom collapsed breathlessly into a chair, trying desperately to make some sense of these events. In the space of a few minutes he had seen several

impossible things – but there seemed to be no choice but to believe them.

'W-what happened to Bart?' asked Janet, close to tears.

Rose sat next to her and took her hand. 'It's too hard for you or me to understand,' she said compassionately. She pointed to the Doctor, who was pacing up and down the length of the billiard table, absent-mindedly scattering the balls with one hand across the baize as he passed. 'He can. Just trust him, he can get you out of this.'

Dr Carr had regained a little of his composure. Ransom watched as he marched up to the Doctor. 'Are you saying that is what happened to Marten and Steiffers?'

The Doctor nodded. 'And to the rest of us, if you don't let me think for a second.'

'You see?' Glenda Neil told Carr, with a kind of weary triumphalism. 'I don't know where you got that nonsense about Kitty Rickshaw or whoever, but you were wrong.'

'Wrong?' Dr Carr rolled this unfamiliar word about on his tongue. 'I hardly think it can be that, no. I was not acquainted with the full facts, by Cicero's beard.'

'Cicero hasn't got a beard,' said Rose casually.

'She's right,' agreed the Doctor, and nobody knew quite what to say to that.

Eventually, Dr Carr raised a self-important finger. 'Doctor, that door is surely of no protection to us against these... demons. They entered the library easily enough.'

'I had figured that out, yeah,' said the Doctor. 'But there was nowhere else to go.'

Ransom's chest tightened. 'You mean the same thing could happen again?'

Before the Doctor could reply, Dr Carr took him by the arm. 'Listen, young man. Perhaps I was mistaken. But I'll tell you something for nothing. If you're after a fellow thinker, I'm your man. Share your problem with me.'

The Doctor gave a grim smile. 'It'd take me about three years to bring you up to speed. We've got, I dunno, minutes.'

Rose left Janet in the arms of her father and gently steered Dr Carr away from the Doctor. 'Let him think, okay?'

Dr Carr shook her off. 'I demand the facts!' he blustered.

Rose sighed. 'All right. There's an alien spaceship right here. The aliens inside are trapped, caught between real space and the time vortex by engine trouble. They're trying to fix it, get out and go home, and every time they try they generate an energy field that kills people.' She paused to absorb Dr Carr's astonished reaction. 'Could you have worked that out?'

'I must admit it would have been rather difficult,' he sighed. He leaned closer to her. 'But I think I've worked *you* out. I knew I would, if I could have a little more time.'

Rose flinched a little. 'What does that mean?'

Dr Carr pointed at her. 'You, my dear, are a shop girl. You're very used to apologising for somebody else's behaviour, and I don't think it's the Doctor's – no, you haven't known him long enough to make sense of that. I'd say it was your mother. You're an only child, and the Doctor is the most stimulating person you've ever met. You pray that you will stay at his side forever. He makes you alive. Also, I think you were perhaps courting a young gentleman, but he wasn't exactly up to scratch.'

Rose swallowed and shivered. 'You're either telepathic or just... very, very scary.'

Dr Carr smiled. 'I am merely a student of human nature. You may possess a most peculiar manner, but I still got you.' He pointed to the Doctor, who was now leant on the far side of the billiard table, twirling the cue over and over in his hands like a bandleader with his baton at a military tattoo. 'Now, he's another matter. Nothing fits...'

Ransom was now so scared and tired that he was prepared to accept anything. And it was a considerable relief that Dr Carr had regained at least some of his stoic self-image. Nobody had ever really got to know old Carr, thought Ransom, not even his own wife, because nobody had seen him vulnerable or defeated. Now he had been very publicly proved wrong, Ransom's heart went out to

him. He looked over at Janet, and found to his delight and astonishment that she was choosing, in this moment of extreme distress, to look back at him. In that flash as their eyes met, they both knew their future, if there was to be one, would be together.

Further considerations were forestalled as the Doctor strode back over to them. 'I've had my thinking time,' he said.

'And what have you thunk?' said Dr Carr rather rudely.

'I don't think the aliens know they're doing it,' said the Doctor. 'I don't think they can see out of the ship. They're stranded somewhere way off course, and they're panicking, switching their drive on and off in random patterns, all over the place, so something – anything – might happen. When a human gets in the way of that energy – *oof*. Now they've gone and trapped us here, but not on purpose. They're just scared.'

'I know what you've thunk,' said Rose. 'You're going to try and talk to them.'

'Yeah.' He produced a slender metallic object from an inside pocket, which looked to Ransom something like an elongated pen torch, and flicked a tiny button on the side. The tip started to glow with an eerie blue light. He thumbed the button repeatedly, so the blue light flickered off and on like a Morse signal. 'That should get through to 'em. I'm using the standard galactic code of the 455th century, everyone knows that.'

'I don't,' grunted Lord Farthingale from the other side of the room.

'Now,' said the Doctor, 'hopefully they'll get this message and – whoa...' He clutched his side. A moment later the ghastly buzzing and swimming in the air returned, only this time centred directly around the Doctor. But instead of being lifted up like Faversham he was surrounded by a shimmering red light.

Ransom was astonished as Rose immediately leapt forward and grabbed the Doctor round the middle. He opened his mouth in protest but no sound could be heard over the dreadful buzz. And a moment later, both the Doctor and Rose vanished along with the red light and the buzz.

Janet ran over, taking Ransom's hand. Even in that supreme moment of terror, he could not help feeling joy at her touch.

'They've gone,' said Glenda Neil rather pointlessly.

Dr Carr grunted. 'Harrumph. Yes. I dare say the aliens picked up the Doctor's signal, and took him aboard their ship. They must be desperate for rescue, like a drowning man clutching at driftwood.' He chuckled. 'I'm rather getting the hang of this, aren't I, Ransom? "Out of my depth" – pshaw!'

ROSE WAS STILL HOLDING ON TO THE DOCTOR several seconds after they rematerialized. She looked up at his face, trying to read his expression. 'Tell me what I'm gonna see when I turn round.'

'Nothing too pretty,' said the Doctor.

Rose sighed, gave herself a moment to prepare, and turned to look.

They were in a small darkened chamber, like an inverted pyramid, which consisted of several pieces of organic growth that she guessed might be instruments of some weird technology. It was lit by a red glow. Rose's attention passed immediately to the three huddled shapes by the far wall. They were tiny alien bodies, vaguely ovoid in shape with floppy vestigial limbs. Each had a large blue stain on its skull.

The Doctor strode over to them. 'The crew. Must have died when the engine went kaput.' He pointed to the stains. 'They were linked telepathically to the ship's computer.'

'So when it crashed it blew out their brains,' Rose surmised. 'Whatever brought us in here was automatic.'

'Yeah, an emergency programme. Kept trying to get the ship going, trying anything, flailing about. And when it picked up the signal it pulled me in here to repair it.'

'It pulled *us* in here,' Rose pointed out.

'Who's the one with the sonic screwdriver?' asked the Doctor. 'And he'd better do the job – then we can get out.' He muttered something at the end of the sentence.

'Was that the word "hopefully"?' asked Rose as the Doctor started work.

THE ATMOSPHERE AT THE HOUSE OF LORD

Farthingale was returning to normal. Stephen Carter had rather bravely left the billiard room and ascertained that there was no trace of any unearthly buzzing or shimmering inside or outside the house. Glenda Neil had, rather unsurprisingly, taken the first available opportunity to spit in Dr Carr's big red face and stomp off into the night. Lord Farthingale was on the phone to the police, trying to work out exactly what he was going to report about the death of Bart Faversham. And Ransom had joined Dr Carr to investigate an extraordinary object that Janet had discovered in her room. It was a tall blue cabinet of some kind with the words POLICE PUBLIC CALL BOX across its top above a pair of grimy windows. Ransom rattled at the door handle but it was firmly locked.

'Ah, yes,' said Dr Carr, squinting at it through his spectacles. 'This is some kind of police telephone post. I've had advance notice of these from my friends at the Yard. Soon they'll be all over the country.'

'But what's it doing in my room? wailed Janet. 'And will

we ever see Rose and the other Doctor again?'

'Well,' said Dr Carr. 'I imagine this box was put here by the police earlier today as a kind of er... spying mechanism.'

'Hardly a very subtle one,' observed Ransom.

'Ah yes, by Cicero's beard,' said Dr Carr. 'As to your second question – I fear young Rose and the good Doctor gave their lives to save ours.' Ransom couldn't help noticing that Dr Carr didn't seem too upset about that. 'We shall never more see that fascinating pair of adventurers.'

'Wrong again!' said a familiar voice. The Doctor and Rose breezed into the bedroom. 'On both questions.'

Rose nodded to the box. 'That's our spaceship, see.'

The sound of a police siren could be heard coming down the valley road. 'Uh-oh, the peelers. We'd better get going,' said the Doctor, unlocking the door of the box.

'Just one moment,' said Dr Carr, turning redder again. He came right up to the Doctor. 'One last try... You're from Lancashire...'

The Doctor shook his head.

'You were married to an older woman...'

'Nope.'

'You have a twin brother...'

Rose laughed. 'Give it up,' she said kindly and led the Doctor inside the box.

A moment later it gave a tremendous groaning sound and simply disappeared before their eyes.

Dr Carr grunted, turned to Ransom and put an arm around his shoulder. 'Listen, old fella. About this case. Going to write it up?'

Janet took Ransom's hand. 'Not on our honeymoon, he won't be.'

Ransom grinned at Dr Carr. 'I'll keep your secret.'

'Good,' said Dr Carr. He blinked owlishly at them, gathered himself together and waddled out of the room. ●

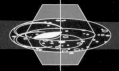

Meet the Doctor

WRITTEN BY RUSSELL T DAVIES

hen the Doctor came to Earth – to track down the Nestene Consciousness and its plastic servants, the Autons – he had no intention of finding a human companion. He'd had fellow travellers alongside him before, of course, and most of them human. His favourite species! But that was in the old days, when the universe seemed young and fresh and more inclined to friendly gestures.

The universe, since then, had changed. At least for the Doctor.

There had been a War, the Great Time War between the Daleks and the Time Lords. There had been two Time Wars before this – the skirmish between the Halldons and the Eternals, and then the brutal slaughter of the Omnicraven Uprising – and on both occasions, the Doctor's people had stepped in to settle the matter. The Time Lords had a policy of non-intervention in the affairs of the universe, but on a higher level, in affairs of the Time Vortex, they had assumed discreetly the role of protectors. They were the self-appointed keepers of the peace. Until forced to fight.

Now, the story of the Great (and final) Time War is hard to piece together, because so little survived. Certainly, both superpowers had been testing each others' strength for many, many years. The Daleks had threatened the Time Lord High Council before, by trying to replace its members with Dalek duplicates. And one of the Dalek Puppet Emperors had openly declared his hostility. Though perhaps the Daleks' wrath was justifiable – they had been provoked! At one point in their history, the Time Lords had actually sent the Doctor back in time, to prevent the creation of the Daleks. An act of genocide! The Time Lords fired the first shot – though in their defence, they took this course of action because they had foreseen a time when the Daleks would overrun all civilised life and become the dominant life-form in the universe.

Some tried to find a peaceful solution. While it's hard to find precise records of these events, it's said that under the Act of Master Restitution, President Romana opened a peace treaty with the Daleks. Others claim that the Etra Prime Incident began the escalation of events. But whatever the cause – and it's almost certain that the full story has yet to be uncovered – the terrible War began. The Time Lords reached back into their own history, to assemble a fleet of Bowships, Black Hole Carriers and N-Forms; the Daleks unleashed the full might of the Deathsmiths of Goth, and launched an awesome fleet into the Vortex, led by the Emperor himself.

The War raged, but for most species in the universe, life continued as normal. The War was fought in the Vortex, and beyond that, in the Ultimate Void, beyond the eyes and ears of ordinary creatures. The Lesser Species lived in ignorance. If a planet found its history subtly changing – perhaps distorting and rewriting itself under the pressures of the rupturing Vortex – then its people were part of that change, and perceived nothing to be wrong. Only the Higher Species – those further up the evolutionary ladder – saw what was happening. The Forest of Cheem gazed upon the bloodshed, and wept. The Nestene Consciousness lost all of its planets, and found itself mutating under temporal stress. The Greater Animus perished and its Carsenome Walls fell

everything he had just done…

He is alone and thinks, somehow, that he deserves this. And as he wanders on, he decides that no one should stand beside him. He's got no room, on board his TARDIS. He is a traveller, and needs no other.

But then he finds himself in the cellar of a London shop at closing time, and he grabs the hand of an

...he finds himself in the cellar of a London shop at closing time, and he grabs the hand of an Earthling called Rose Tyler

into dust. And it is said that the Eternals themselves watched, and despaired of this reality, and fled their hallowed halls, never to be seen again…

Years passed, as the mighty armies clashed. And then, silence. No one knows exactly what happened in the final battle. And no one knows how it came to end. All that is known is that one man strode from the wreckage, one man walked free from the ruins of Gallifrey and Skaro. The Time Lord called the Doctor. And his hearts were heavy as he boarded his ship once more, and took to the skies, to escape everything he had just seen;

Earthling called Rose Tyler, and looks into her eyes, and all those resolutions go out of the window! The journey goes on, with a human at his side, and who knows where it will end…

And far away, across the universe, on the planet Crafe Tec Heydra, one side of a mountain carries carvings and hieroglyphs, crude representations of an invisible War. The artwork shows two races clashing, one metal, one flesh; a fearsome explosion; and a solitary survivor walking from the wreckage. Solitary? Perhaps not. Under this figure, a phrase has been scratched in the stone, which translates as: *you are not alone...* ●

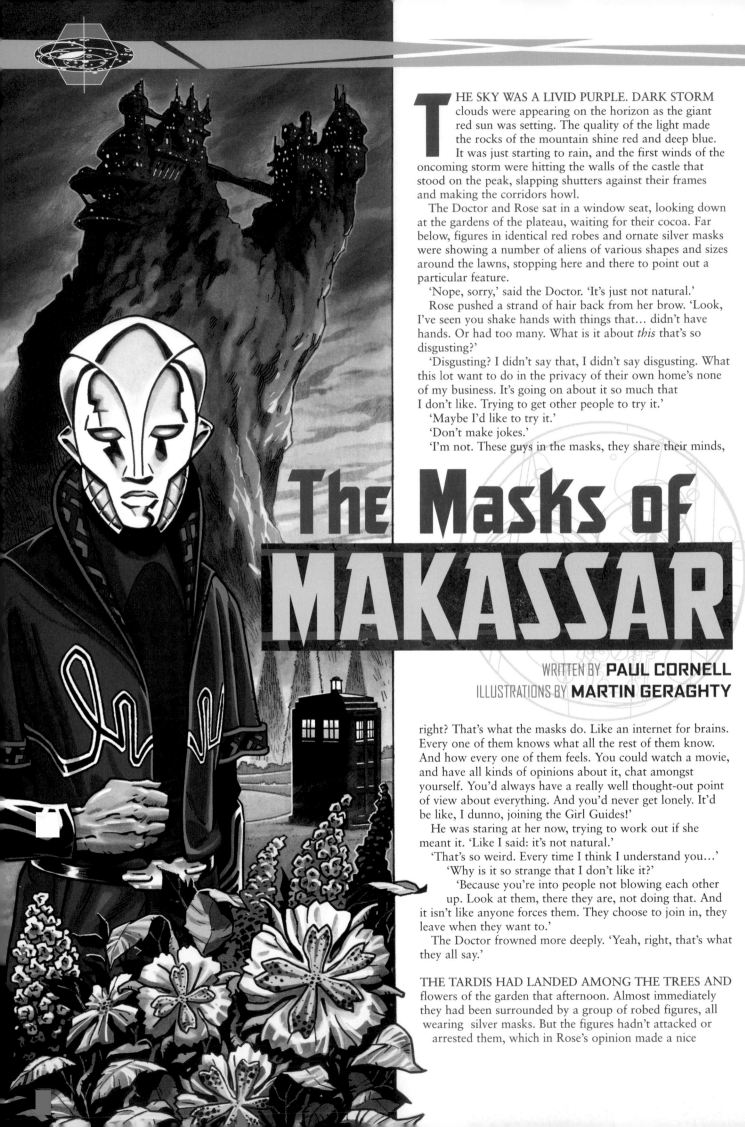

THE SKY WAS A LIVID PURPLE. DARK STORM clouds were appearing on the horizon as the giant red sun was setting. The quality of the light made the rocks of the mountain shine red and deep blue. It was just starting to rain, and the first winds of the oncoming storm were hitting the walls of the castle that stood on the peak, slapping shutters against their frames and making the corridors howl.

The Doctor and Rose sat in a window seat, looking down at the gardens of the plateau, waiting for their cocoa. Far below, figures in identical red robes and ornate silver masks were showing a number of aliens of various shapes and sizes around the lawns, stopping here and there to point out a particular feature.

'Nope, sorry,' said the Doctor. 'It's just not natural.'

Rose pushed a strand of hair back from her brow. 'Look, I've seen you shake hands with things that... didn't have hands. Or had too many. What is it about *this* that's so disgusting?'

'Disgusting? I didn't say that, I didn't say disgusting. What this lot want to do in the privacy of their own home's none of my business. It's going on about it so much that I don't like. Trying to get other people to try it.'

'Maybe I'd like to try it.'

'Don't make jokes.'

'I'm not. These guys in the masks, they share their minds,

The Masks of
MAKASSAR

WRITTEN BY **PAUL CORNELL**
ILLUSTRATIONS BY **MARTIN GERAGHTY**

right? That's what the masks do. Like an internet for brains. Every one of them knows what all the rest of them know. And how every one of them feels. You could watch a movie, and have all kinds of opinions about it, chat amongst yourself. You'd always have a really well thought-out point of view about everything. And you'd never get lonely. It'd be like, I dunno, joining the Girl Guides!'

He was staring at her now, trying to work out if she meant it. 'Like I said: it's not natural.'

'That's so weird. Every time I think I understand you...'

'Why is it so strange that I don't like it?'

'Because you're into people not blowing each other up. Look at them, there they are, not doing that. And it isn't like anyone forces them. They choose to join in, they leave when they want to.'

The Doctor frowned more deeply. 'Yeah, right, that's what they all say.'

THE TARDIS HAD LANDED AMONG THE TREES AND flowers of the garden that afternoon. Almost immediately they had been surrounded by a group of robed figures, all wearing silver masks. But the figures hadn't attacked or arrested them, which in Rose's opinion made a nice

change. In fact they'd been quite friendly, taken them up to the castle above, fed them, and introduced their leader, Makassar. He told them all about the masks, what they could do, how they linked the people of this planet. How much good they had done. He'd been eager, almost excited to explain the principles, the benefits. But the Doctor had grown more and more quiet. A whole range of galactic imperial leaders were arriving that day, Makassar had said, invited here to examine the mask technology, and to decide amongst themselves whether they wanted to take it away with them, to benefit their own races. As Makassar explained, he didn't want the masks getting into the wrong hands, being used for evil. The Doctor had said nothing.

'THEY EVEN WANT YOU TO SIT IN ON THEIR conference.' Rose said. 'That's pretty flattering.'

The Doctor snorted. 'Yeah, and why d'you think that is?'

'Because they think you being a Time Lord is a big deal.'

'Well if you hadn't told 'em…'

'Makassar asked!' Rose was getting annoyed. 'It was hardly 'tell me your origins, pitiful creatures'. He just asked where we came from! Fair enough question. You didn't say *not* to tell.'

'Didn't say you should, either,' muttered the Doctor.

Rose gave him a look. 'They've been really nice. If only they could hear what you're saying about them…'

'Your cocoa.'

They both turned at the calm voice from the doorway. It was one of the Units. There was no telling how long he (or she, the robes seldom gave you a clue, and the voice was always the same) had been standing there. The silver mask was the same for every one of them, a bland set of male features, with blank eyes and a mouth that was always set in the same, neutral expression.

The Doctor quickly got up and took the tray with two mugs on it from the Unit. 'Right, thanks, ta.'

The Unit bowed and left once more.

The Doctor brought the tray back to the window seat. He held up a hand to stop Rose from talking until they heard the footsteps in the corridor fade into the distance. Then he lifted his cup and sniffed the dark liquid carefully.

Rose glared at him, blew on her cocoa and took a quick sip. 'It's all right, it's just –' Her expression became a frown. 'Wait a sec.' She put down her cup. 'Must… obey… Makassar. Must… kill… Doctor!'

The Doctor knocked away her outstretched fingers and shook his head. 'Yeah, yeah. Very funny I don't think.'

Rose was trying to stop herself laughing, her hands to her mouth. 'You should have seen your face, just for a second!'

'Listen. The real reason they want me at their conference is because I'd give it a bit of moral authority. A Time Lord saying it's okay. The Time Lords used to stick their noses into stuff like this, stop it happening.'

'So they got shirty about linking up brains too? Why?'

'Nah, they weren't against it cos of that. They had somethin' similar themselves, to keep their minds in after they died. But they let it make a lot of their decisions for them, and they didn't like anyone else –'

'Oh! *That's* why.' Rose slapped herself on the forehead.

'What are you on about?'

'This reminds you of home. Of how it was run.'

The Doctor frowned, raised a finger as if to make an important point, then lowered it again, his eyes flicking away, lost for words.

She continued, not mocking now, but more gently. 'It reminds you of what you ran away from.'

'I never said I ran away. Why would I run away?'

'Because it was like this, and you didn't want to join in.' She grinned. 'I've got it right, haven't I?'

The Doctor put down his cup without having touched a drop. 'Okay. So I didn't want to be one of the herd. No surprise that I still don't then, is it? Nothing wrong with that. You don't have to look so smug about it either.' He stood up and went to the door. 'It's getting dark. We'll go down the mountain and get back to the TARDIS in the morning.'

'What about the conference?'

'They can take their conference and –' He slapped the side of the doorframe. 'And come to some really well thought out conclusions. Night.'

And he was gone.

Rose sighed. 'Just cos I'm right.'

THE DOCTOR MARCHED ALONG the corridor, turned a corner, and was nearly back to his room, when he stopped. He was feeling annoyed with himself. What Rose had said was true: he did pride himself on meeting beings

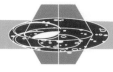

that didn't look like he did and treating them all alike, as friends until he knew differently. There were a few exceptions to that, but those were based on first-hand experience, on knowing that certain species really *were* always out to get you.

Makassar and his mates in the masks had been nothing but kind to them. So keen to talk with the Doctor, so enthusiastic about his creations. And the man was dying. He hadn't told the Doctor that until Rose had been shown to her room. He hadn't wanted to upset her. Then he'd found cocoa beans for them in his garden of alien flora. And still the Doctor treated him with suspicion.

He heard the voice of Makassar from downstairs. Explaining something to the representatives. The Doctor came to a decision. He was being a git, and there were only two things to do when that happened: sulk (and he'd already done that), and then do something to make it better.

He put on his best smile and determinedly headed downstairs.

MAKASSAR WAS TALLER THAN MOST OF THE UNITS. He wore an identical red robe, but his mask was bigger than all the others. It was also, judging by the painting that stood over the fireplace in the main hall of the castle, an accurate representation of the facial features underneath.

'Spokesperson, not leader,' Makassar was saying to the tall figure of Repthon, one of the blue-fronded Intransigents of Smorg. They were never the easiest people to talk to, recalled the Doctor. 'This mind,' he continued, pointing to himself, 'is not their leader, merely the spokesperson for the group mind.' A group of the Units, gathered with the alien representatives in the great hall, all bowed their heads in agreement at the same moment. Goblets of various drinks hung in the air in front of the assembled aliens, held there by the impressive telekinetic powers of Makassar's people.

'But your mask is bigger,' gurgled Repthon. 'Why is this?'

'It serves as the processing centre for the thoughts of the group mind,' replied Makassar. 'Without it, we could not perform feats such as this.' He pointed, and the huge table around which they had earlier convened floated into the air.

'Nice one!' the Doctor thought this an appropriate moment for some friendly applause. 'Must make the hoovering a lot easier.'

Makassar turned at the sound. The table fell to the ground with a colossal thump.

Everyone coughed and looked aside, embarrassed.

The Doctor made himself grin a notch more.

'Doctor, we are pleased that you have decided to join us.' The Units bowed again at Makassar's words. 'You were reserved earlier, uncommunicative. Your body language spoke of discomfort with the society we have established here.'

'You don't miss a trick, do you Makassar? Nah, don't mind me. I was just in a mood.'

'That is good news. And please, call this mind Akimus. That was this mind's first name.'

'Akimus.' The Doctor smiled, pleased he was doing his best. 'Okay. So, anything been decided, Akimus?'

us,' it managed. 'Help...' and the next word took a real effort, '*me!*'

'Who are you?'

'My name is... my name...' The spectre twisted in the air, its ghostly form seemingly wracked with pain.

Then, with a terrible scream, it launched itself at Rose. She yelled as its hands went straight through her, and turned, relieved that it couldn't hurt her.

Only to have the cocoa cup from her bedside table lift into the air and smash into the side of her head.

The ghost floated into her view, raced at her, trying to hit her again. She threw out a hand, which went right through it. The bedclothes were rising around her, grabbing at her hand, wrapping around her, reaching up to enfold her neck, her face, her mouth –

'Doctor!' she bellowed. '*Doctor!*'

THE DOCTOR AND MAKASSAR were sitting by the fireplace in two vast chairs, sharing a bottle of fine brandy, alone now the alien delegates had all retired. The Doctor had been listening to the scientist, and, to his relief, a lot of the unease he'd felt around the masked Units had vanished. All it had taken was to have a bit of a chat. But as he looked over at his host, he noticed that Makassar's was holding his masked head in his hands, his whole body trembling. 'You all right?'

Makassar raised a hand in apology and shook his head. 'This body's condition... it fails this mind sometimes.'

ROSE HEAVED AGAINST THE TIGHTNESS OF THE sheets wrapped around her and flung herself out of bed, determined to make it to the door.

But as she did so, the bedclothes billowed out away from her, and she landed in a crumpled heap, panting. Nothing clutching at her, no ghost in the room.

She carefully sat up and looked around.

It was as if the pleading spectre, and its puzzling, sudden attack, had all been a dream.

She got unsteadily to her feet, and started to pull on her clothes.

THE DOCTOR HAD CHECKED MAKASSAR'S PULSE, and was watching his swift, pained breathing. 'You know, there are places where the medicine's much more advanced than in this bit of the galaxy. I could give you a lift, get you sorted out.'

'No, no...' Makassar made a visible effort, and his breathing slowed. 'This body and mind are not important, only the group mind. That was why this mind began this, to make people see, make species see... how much better being together is. An end to war, to conflict of all kinds...'

The Doctor shrugged. 'I'm with you on the principle, mate. But maybe not the methods.'

ROSE HAD THOUGHT FOR A WHILE about popping back downstairs and seeing what the aliens were up too. She'd seen a lot of strange beings during her travels with the Doctor, and usually she couldn't get enough of them. But tiredness at the end of a very long day had finally got the better of her and she'd gone to bed, pulling the light but nicely warm sheets right over her head and burying herself in the vastly comfortable pillows. She was sure that tomorrow the Doctor would open up a bit more, that she'd find out more about him, maybe more about his strange home planet. That was always something to look forward to.

And then she was asleep.

She wasn't sure what woke her, hours later when all was dark and silent. She opened her eyes without being aware of hearing a sound.

And realised that she was looking at something. It was one of the masks, right in front of her face.

She jumped up, pulling at the covers. 'Hey!' she shouted. 'What are you doing?'

The mask rose with her.

She suddenly realised that it wasn't connected to the body of a Unit. Or if it was, the body was that of a ghost, just a faint outline. Even the mask itself wasn't quite solid. She could see right through it.

'Okay, what are you doing here...? What's going on?!'

She was shocked when the mouth of the phantom mask started to move, as if struggling to produce words. 'Help...

ROSE LOOKED CAUTIOUSLY OUT OF HER DOOR, then stepped into the corridor.

She'd taken a few steps when she heard something behind her… and turned to see a Unit running down the corridor towards her.

Rose ran to the junction. And saw another Unit coming the other way. Only one way left. She took it, sprinting as fast as she could.

She realised a second too late that it was a trap. Two Units stepped out from two doors on opposite sides of the corridor.

One of them had a mask in his hands.

'No!' she shouted.

They grabbed her. Rose fought. They seized all her limbs.

Slowly, the Unit pushed the mask towards her face. Powerful hands held her head in place, to stop her thrashing. The darkness descended over her.

'YOU THINK WE CAN AGREE TO DISAGREE?' Makassar suddenly, surprisingly, laughed, a note of cruelty creeping into his voice. 'Oh! This mind doesn't think you understand at all! But now that all the alien representatives are safely accounted for, you will. It is time for us to begin.'

The Doctor looked up, and realised that a group of Units had entered the room, covering all the exits. One of them held a mask in his hands.

The Doctor leapt up from his chair and ran at one of the doors.

They were ready, they grabbed him. He knocked one of them off his feet, then another, but in the end they brought him down.

Makassar stood over him. He held the mask in his hands. He pushed it down onto the Doctor's face. 'You will understand, Doctor, when this mind leaves its frail body and takes yours!'

ROSE BLINKED. SLOWLY, SHE TURNED ON THE SPOT.

She was standing in front of the 24-hour shop, near where she lived. Only, certain things were different. *Really* different…

The Doctor walked round the corner, grinned and pointed at her. 'Told ya!'

'Where are we?'

'Makassar's using all the power of his group mind to try and invade my brain. So I grabbed you out of his mental clutches, and made us somewhere to hide. I made it out of my memories, but somewhere you'd feel at home. What d'you think?'

'What do I think? You remember us living in mud huts?'

He frowned. 'Don't you? What, none at all?'

Rose shook her head patiently.

The Doctor closed his eyes and concentrated. The buildings around them became slightly more modern, though there was still the occasional thatched roof visible. 'How about that?'

'Never mind. How do we get out of this?'

'Not a clue. He wants to use my body to put his mind in. And, you know, what with him being actually *bad* and all, and not this amazing benevolent philanthropist who wants to bring peace to the universe –'

Rose, jabbed him with her elbow. 'Yeah, great, so you were right to be a bigot. That will *so* comfort me during my horrible death.'

'I'll bet he's put the alien representatives into masks as well. They take them home, they catch on, he's got more and more power, more and more minds to work with…'

'So he's not just one of the gang, he's actually in charge.

That mask of his isn't just some kind of central point, it controls all the others.'

The Doctor was looking round, as if he'd just heard something. A moment later, Rose heard it too. The sound of marching feet.

Around the corner, into the shopping area of the estate, came an army of Units. Hundreds of them. All masked, all looking exactly the same. Except for the figure that led them, Makassar himself, his bigger mask shining with energy.

'They've found us!' The Doctor grabbed Rose's hand and ran.

THEY RAN TO ROSE'S FLAT. WHICH, ROSE NOTED, had a really detailed front door and not much apart from that. The Doctor grabbed the door and heaved it open.

Rose was surprised – and also quite surprised that anything now could surprise her – to find her Mum standing in the hall. Really quite an accurate version of Jackie, too.

'What?' she looked at them, astonished. 'What's going on?'

'Oh no,' the Doctor pointed at her. 'I didn't imagine you!' With one blow, he sent her flying. Her body hit the wall, reverted to its true form of a Unit, and spun out through the wall via a trick panel that the Doctor must have just conjured up. 'I didn't think they'd had time, but while you were in the group mind, they must have raided your memories too. They'll know where we are all the time.'

'Should have used your own memories.'

'Harder to get you into those. It'd take too much energy.'

'Can we stop 'em getting in?'

The Doctor ran into the lounge, looking around desperately. 'Doubt it. I'm trickier than them, I've been running rings round 'em, but they're a hell of a lot stronger. If we get into a straight fight I'm toast.'

A thought suddenly struck Rose, and she put a hand on the Doctor's shoulder.

'Is this about how you're feeling?' she frowned. 'I mean, this must be a complete nightmare for you, these guys trying to make you into one of the crowd –'

'Ta for reminding me, yeah, this is about me holding on with my fingertips against a huge enemy that wants to swallow me up, and I think it just might, cos I can't think of a thing to stop it.'

Rose suddenly smiled. 'And you still took a second to save me first?'

He smiled back. 'Regretting it already.'

Rose looked around the blank room, desperately trying to think of a way to help, some solution. 'That lot outside,' she said at last, 'can't all be together. There was this guy, this ghost kind of thing. He asked for my help, like he was trying to get out… and then he attacked me.'

The Doctor was staring at her. 'Makassar must have exerted his control, got him back into line, made him do that. So that single mind… he's got a connection to you. He'd recognise you. And he managed to send his mental energy out into the real world, to create a ghost image of himself…' He put his hands on her shoulders. 'Rose… how would you feel about doing something really scary?'

ROSE TOOK A DEEP BREATH, AND STEPPED OUT into the estate.

There were Units everywhere, standing in vast armies filling up every road, looking down from every roof and walkway. Makassar stood at the front of them.

Rose raised her hand. 'Erm, hi! We've met, haven't we?' She searched the crowd for any sign of difference, any movement at all.

'Take her,' said Makassar. 'Return her to the group mind.' As one, the Units moved forward…

IN THE LOUNGE OF ROSE'S FLAT, THE DOCTOR stood, his eyes closed, concentrating hard.

'That's it,' he whispered. 'Go after her, let your guard down…'

ROSE MADE HERSELF STAY WHERE SHE WAS AS they closed in. 'Hey, it's me! Rose. Remember me? Whichever of you it was that tried to get free, that tried to talk to me… You've gotta try again!'

Amongst the army, a single figure stopped moving. He swayed on his feet, as if just the effort of standing still was taking all his energy.

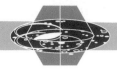

'That's it!' shouted Rose. 'Fight him! All of you, fight!' The army all turned to look at the rebel Unit.

'YES!' SHOUTED THE DOCTOR. 'WE'RE OFF!'
And his mind leapt free.

HE WAS SUDDENLY RUSHING THROUGH THE corridors of the castle, his body transparent, moving fast as a ghost. He knew he didn't have long before Makassar realised he'd left their mental battle and would overwhelm Rose.

But he didn't need long.

Ahead of him was the hall of the castle, where the great fireplace stood. The alien representatives once more assembled there, except now each one of them had a mask over its face, or what it had instead of a face. Surrounding them stood a mass of Units. All of them were perfectly still, lost in the mental conflict.

And in their midst stood Makassar. The Doctor's phantom body rushed closer and closer to him. Still he didn't move. Just a few more seconds...

Makassar lashed out with his hand.

The Doctor was expecting the blow. He ducked under it. With one thought, his ghostly hands were solid. He grabbed the mask of one of the Units. And pulled.

The man screamed as the mask was wrenched from his face. He fell, unconscious, as all the other Units staggered.

'You have only moments!' Makassar yelled. 'Freeing one of my servants will not stop the power of the group mind!'

IT TOOK ROSE A MOMENT TO REALISE WHAT HAD happened. Makassar had blinked out, vanished, which was bad news because that meant he was dealing with the Doctor back in the real world.

But the army of Units was swaying, disconcerted, starting to mill about. Rose knew what to do. 'Who are you?!' she yelled. 'All of you! Tell me your names!'

IT WAS A GREAT EFFORT FOR THE DOCTOR TO EVEN keep the mask in the air with his ghostly hands. He heaved it towards Makassar.

'In a moment I will consume the mind of your friend, Doctor! But first I will deal with you!' Makassar thrust one gloved hand into the centre of the Doctor's ghostly body. The other grabbed the mask in his hand. Mental battle was joined once more.

The Doctor roared in anger and pain. 'It's an old song, Makassar! The power of the many? What about the power of just one?'

With his free hand, he snatched for Makassar's mask.

Makassar fought, grabbing his own mask with both hands, holding it to his face.

The Doctor heaved with every iota of his will. It was a will that had gotten used to being alone, that had gotten used to fighting for the things of the few against the things of the many. And it was enough.

With a yell of triumph, he hauled Makassar's mask away from his face.

Beneath was the very white skin of a frightened old man, his eyes screwed up against the light. 'I– I can still control them! My will is supreme! This mind –'

'Ah, control yerself!'

The Doctor shoved the Unit's mask onto Makassar's face.

ROSE STARED AS, ALL AROUND HER, FIRST THE army of Units and then the buildings began to fade.

Then there was a moment of darkness and fear.

And then the Doctor lifted the mask from her face and she could see him grinning down at her. He helped her to her feet, her mind back in her body again, both of them in the great hall of the castle.

'Wake up, Rose,' he said. 'No napping on this job.'

'What happened?' she asked. All around, Units sat or lay, their masks in their hands, laughing or weeping, or just staring into space. The alien representatives were gathered, looking stunned, examining the masks that had once imprisoned them.

'They're all free.'

Rose saw one of the former Units looking at her. She ran over to him. 'You're my ghost, aren't you?'

He took her hand in his. 'My name is Eln. Thank you, you freed us all.'

'Mate, it was you who tipped us off.'

Rose stood again to see the Doctor smiling down at the man. 'What about Makassar?'

The Doctor led her to a corner, where Makassar lay curled in a foetal position. The smaller mask of a Unit was fixed on his face. 'He's out to lunch.'

'I must obey...' Makassar was muttering. 'I must obey... myself. But I must give orders... but I must obey...'

'Trapped in a loop,' the Doctor said. 'When everyone sorts themselves out, they can take the mask off and hand him over to the law.'

'Poor guy,' whispered Rose.

The Doctor looked hard at her for a moment, then broke into a grin. 'Rose Tyler,' he said. 'You never cease to amaze me!' ●

C'MON, NOBODY'S *NOBODY*, Y'KNOW!

HELLO, I'M *THE DOCTOR!*

WHO? HOW DID YOU --

I SPOTTED YOU ORBITIN' EARTH AND THOUGHT I'D POKE MY HEAD IN THE DOOR -- I'M THE OFFICIAL *WELCOME WAGON* FOR ALL ALIEN VISITS!

SO -- *COURTROOM,* EH? *FANTASTIC!*

I HEREBY DECLARE MY STATUS AS A *LEGAL REPRESENTATIVE* OF THE *HYPER-TEMPORAL MAGISTRATE AUTHORITY,* AS SHOWN ON THIS *OFFICIAL BADGE* OF OFFICE WHICH YOU CAN ALL *PLAINLY SEE...*

I WISH TO ACT AS *DEFENCE COUNSEL* FOR THIS *EARTHLING!*

THIS IS NOT A *TRIAL.* SHOGALATH'S *GUILT* IS *UNQUESTIONABLE.*

MAYBE, BUT HIS *IDENTITY* ISN'T! I MEAN, *VANDOS* HAS GOTTA BE A GOOD *SIXTY THOUSAND LIGHT YEARS* FROM EARTH! HOW CAN *THIS* BLOKE BE SHOGALATH? AND ISN'T HE *DEAD* BY NOW?

HE *IS* SHOGALATH... THERE IS NO DOUBT...

FOR *FIVE DECADES* I HAVE CAST THE *QUANTUM RUNES* IN PREPARATION FOR THIS DAY...

I HAVE *DIVINED* THE *PRECISE POINT* IN *TIME* AND *SPACE* WHEN SHOGALATH'S *SPIRIT* RE-ENTERED THE *PHYSICAL PLANE* -- IN YOUR TONGUE, "3.50 PM, JAN-U-ARY 7TH, 1979, PECK-HAM HOS-PIT-AL"...

YOU ARE THE *REINCARNATION* OF SHOGALATH...

AND UNDER *VANDOSIAN LAW,* YOU SHALL BE BROUGHT TO ACCOUNT FOR ALL OF YOUR *PAST CRIMES!*

COME AGAIN?

YOU *CAN* REMEMBER THE WAY BACK TO THE *TARDIS*, RIGHT? THIS PLACE IS WORSE THAN THE *CROYDON IKEA!*

DON'T WORRY, I'M PART *HOMIN'* PIGEON!

PHIL, YOU'RE *SLOWIN'* US *DOWN!* DROP THE *BUCKET!*

HHHUHH! HHHUHH!

N-NO! IT'S -- HHUHH! -- *COMPANY PROPERTY!* I'LL -- I'LL GET IN *TROUBLE!*

AND PEOPLE CALL ME A NUTTER! *DROP... THE... BUCKET!*

I CAN'T... GO ON...

TOO MUCH...

OH, *MAGIC!* YEAH, LET'S ALL STOP FOR A *CUPPA* AND A *CURRANT BUN!* MIND YOU DON'T SCRATCH YOUR *BUCKET!*

WILL YOU *SHUT UP* FOR FIVE SECONDS? HE'S IN *SHOCK!* THAT'S THE ONLY PIECE OF THE *REAL WORLD* HE CAN STILL *TOUCH* RIGHT NOW...

JUST GIVE ME A MINUTE...

HI, PHIL. MY NAME'S *ROSE.*

H-HELLO...

TONIGHT'S GETTING A BIT *MENTAL*, EH? BELIEVE ME, I KNOW *EXACTLY* HOW YOU FEEL. IT'S LIKE BEING STUCK ON A *MERRY-GO-ROUND* THAT KEEPS GETTING *FASTER* AND *FASTER*, AM I RIGHT?

YEAH...

TELL YOU WHAT...

HOLD MY *HAND.* WE'LL RUN *TOGETHER*, OKAY?

OKAY...

THERE Y'GO! SEE? *TOLD* YOU I COULD --

DOCTOR! THOSE *SQUID-THINGS* --

OUCH. TALK ABOUT AN *OWN GOAL*...

BEFORE I SHOWED MY FACE IN THE COURTROOM, I HAD A *FIDDLE* WITH THEIR *OFFENSIVE SYSTEMS*... JUST IN *CASE*. IF THEY DECIDED TO GET *NASTY* -- BANG -- *BACKFIRE*.

WHAT IF *MORE* OF THOSE CREATURES COME?

OH, THOSE WEREN'T YOUR *TYPICAL* VANDOSIANS. THE *PROPER* ONES ARE A *LOT* FRIENDLIER...

SHOGALATH'S FOLLOWERS GAVE *THOSE* KINDA LOONIES THE BOOT *CENTURIES* AGO. THEY MUST'VE BEEN THE LAST MEMBERS OF SOME LEFTOVER *CULT*.

THIS WAS SHOGALATH.

HE LED A *PEACEFUL REVOLT* WHICH TOPPLED THE CORRUPT VANDOSIAN IMPERIUM. HE WAS LIKE *GANDHI* OR *KING* -- AN *INSPIRATION* TO *BILLIONS*.

HE WAS NO *MONSTER*, PHIL...

HE WAS A *HERO*.

THEY SAID HE WAS A *MONSTER*...

SOON...

DOCTOR... ROSE... *THANK YOU*. I'LL NEVER BE ABLE TO *REPAY* YOU FOR WHAT YOU'VE DONE FOR ME...

YOU SAVED MY LIFE...

IN MORE WAYS THAN *ONE*.

I KNOW THOSE VANDOS BLOKES WERE SHORT OF A FULL QUID...

BUT COULD THEY HAVE BEEN *RIGHT*? COULD PHIL REALLY BE *SHOGALATH*? IS REINCARNATION... Y'KNOW... *REAL*?

MEET *PHIL TYSON*.

HE NOW KNOWS *THE FUTURE* IS NOT SOMETHING YOU *WAIT* FOR...

IT'S SOMETHING YOU GO AND *FIND*.

Y'MEAN, COULD A MAN *DIE* AND HAVE HIS SPIRIT *REBORN* IN A *NEW BODY*?

S'POSE *ANYTHING'S* POSSIBLE...

THE END

THE VAN STATTEN CODE

Named after Henry Van Statten, the famous billionaire philanthropist who mysteriously disappeared in 2012, this code was broken when the so-called Slitheen Tablet was discovered. The Slitheen Tablet gives the same message in both English and the code, thus providing the means to translate other 'Van Statten' documents.

Using your decoding skills, use the Slitheen Tablet solution to decode the message that has just arrived at UNIT Headquarters in Geneva.

Check your translation on page 62...

Looking for cheap spacedrive fission material? The Slitheen family of Raxacoricofallapatorius are pleased to offer a major new refuelling station in the vicinity of the planet formerly known as Earth. Beware of imitations.

INITIATION TEST

U.N.I.T

To join the United Nations Intelligence Taskforce you must be capable of lateral as well as logical thinking.

The questions below are taken from the most recent UNIT Aptitude Test - see how you get on. But beware, the answers are not always quite what you might expect...

- How many letters are there in The Dalek Alphabet?
- If it takes one Auton ten minutes to fill a bath using both taps, how long will it take two Autons to fill the same bath using one tap?
- What is deadly and invisible?
- Raxacoricofallapatorius is the home planet of the Slitheen family, but can you spell it?

Answers on page 62...

Lost Luggage

The Doctor has mislaid his Retrieval Tag on Platform One and can't get the TARDIS back from storage without it. But if he can correctly answer some questions about his ship, the newly-appointed Chief Steward will authorise its return.

Can you help the Doctor answer these questions about the TARDIS? Check your answers on page 62...

- ▶ What colour is the TARDIS?
- ▶ What does it say on the sign at the top of the TARDIS?
- ▶ Which of the doors at the front has a handle?
- ▶ Which door has the lock?
- ▶ Do the doors open inwards or outwards?
- ▶ How many panes of glass are there in each of the TARDIS windows?
- ▶ What does TARDIS stand for?

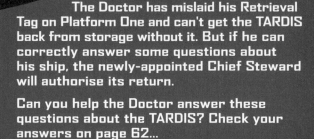

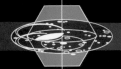

Meet Rose

WRITTEN BY RUSSELL T DAVIES

Rose Marion Tyler was born on 27 April, 1987. Her father, Peter, died on the 7 November of that year, run down by a car outside a local church on the wedding day of Stuart Hoskins and Sarah Clark. So Rose was brought up by her mother, Jacqueline, known to one and all as Jackie. They lived at Flat 48, Bucknall House, Powell Estate, London SE15 7GO, where Jackie made a living by hairdressing from home

Rose always dreamt of travelling, but the furthest she ever got was France, when she was 13, on a school trip. And that ended in disaster – on the day they were meant to visit the Musee de Louvre, Rose and her best mate Shareen Costello escaped the teachers, crossed town, and got on the train to Parc Asterix instead. The police caught them in the queue for the Menhir Express, and Rose and Shareen were sent home – which ruined Mrs Kissock's trip, too, since she had to accompany them on the return journey – and that was the end of Rose's travels. Jackie would take her to Tenby on the South Wales coast for one week every year, but that was it.

When she was 14, Rose started going out with a local lad called Mickey Smith, who lived in the same block of flats, though she always maintained 'it's nothing special'. At 15, Rose was suspended for 3 days from Jericho Street Comprehensive, for persuading the school choir to go on strike. Things got a little better in the summer of that school year – Rose sat her GCSEs, and didn't do too badly – one A, two Bs, four Cs and a D in science. She planned to sit A-Levels in English, French and Art, but then, in September, she made the mistake of falling in love with Jimmy Stone. Jimmy was 20, played bass guitar in a local band called No Hot Ashes, and was officially Fittest Boy on the Estate. Rose fell head over heels. She dumped

Mickey, dropped out of school, moved out of home, and lived in a bedsit with Jimmy Stone. Five months later, she was back home, crying in Jackie's arms, miserable, heartbroken and £800 in debt, while Jimmy was in a camper van to Amsterdam with a woman called Noosh. But Mickey Smith was waiting for Rose, patient and uncomplaining and forgiving.

Rose started working, to pay off the debt. Her first job was behind the till in the Christmas Shop on Clifton's Parade, but six months later, Jackie – calling in a favour from an old boyfriend, Geoff Moon – got her a job in the rather posh Henrik's Department Store. Rose quickly worked her way up from the stock room to the shop floor, and while the job bored her to tears, she felt that she had a duty, to pay her mother ren   earn her way in the world.

And then, one day, Rose's shop blew up, she met an alien called the Doctor, and she discovered that the universe was so much bigger than work and mum and Shareen and jobs and debts and shopping on a budget, getting the bus home, eating chips

Cardiff in 1869; to Platform One in the year Five Billion; to Utah in 2012, to fight a Dalek; to Downing Street, to encounter the Slitheen; to Satellite Five in the future Earth Empire; to World War Two and beyond. There are even books, chronicling her adventures in 1920s London, her trials on the Justicia Penal System, and fighting the war against the Mantodeans, with more stories to come. The adventures go on and on, never stopping.

And maybe, just maybe, Rose Tyler has fallen in love again, although that's a secret she isn't telling anyone just yet. But she trusts the Doctor

Rose ran off with a man she hardly knew, a man with two hearts, to travel in time and space in his miraculous TARDIS

and washing the smell of grease out of   eans. Oh, so much bigger. Mickey was dumped again! Once more, Rose ran off with a man she hardly knew, a man with two hearts, to travel in time and space in his miraculous TARDIS.

In some ways, her life hasn't changed – her wallet's still empty, mum's still nagging and complaining back at home, and poor Mickey Smith is still patient, still uncomplaining, still forgiving. And Jimmy Stone went to prison for 18 months and now sells brushes, door-to-door. But as for Rose – now, every day, when she wakes up, she doesn't know where she's going to be! She's been to

completely. He could do anything – take her to the edge of the universe, dangle her over a clifftop, or even… Even change his face, maybe. Whatever happens, Rose, an ordinary shop girl from London, is having the trip of her lifetime. And the story is by no means over. Her journey is just beginning. Perhaps there's an even greater destiny, waiting, out there, amongst the stars… ●

WRITTEN BY
ROBERT SHEARMAN
ILLUSTRATIONS BY
DARYL JOYCE

Pitter-patter

HE DAY THAT ANDY BECAME A SPACEMAN was the day that Daddy lost his job as a television set salesman.

'They've laid us all off,' he had said when he came home – hours late, his dinner ruined. 'There's no interest in television any more.' His eyes were sparkling, and he was grinning widely. That puzzled Andy – surely this was bad news? Certainly in the last few weeks he'd spied on his Mummy and Daddy sitting downstairs – secretly, when they thought he was asleep – and they'd never *looked* very happy, had they? Daddy drinking that smelly liquor from the drinks cabinet, Mummy crying.

Daddy's breath smelled of that smelly liquor now. Mummy said softly, 'Andy, you should go to bed.'

'No, let him hear this, this affects him as well.' Mummy rescued the dregs of Daddy's dinner and heated it up. Daddy was still grinning as he tucked into his meat-flavoured syrup, talking so excitedly that Andy couldn't help but focus more upon the little droplets of food he'd spit out when he made a particularly enthusiastic point than on the enthusiastic points themselves. 'Actually, it's a blessing. A chance to do something so much more worthwhile. We'll make a lot more money out there, better quality of life for all of us. And it's not as if we're leaving

much behind, is it? What's Earth ever done for us?' Still grinning from ear to ear.

Mummy wasn't grinning. She was crying again. Daddy ignored her.

'You understand, Andy? We're going into space. A whole new planet! Being pioneers! Just like in the westerns. You know, the western films you like on the telly?'

Andy didn't like the westerns. Some of them were in black and white, and most of them were in 2-D. Really, Daddy's bosses were right – there *was* no interest in television any more.

'Your Uncle Bernard says there's a job for me on one of the colony worlds. Mining, something like that. What do you think, Andy? We're going to live out in the stars!' Grinning away still, still spitting out meat-flavoured syrup.

'But you hate Bernard. You always say you hate him,' wept Mummy.

'Well, I like him now.'

Within a week they were all packed and ready to be flown out. Mummy would complain that she'd miss all her friends, but Andy didn't care much – he didn't *have* any friends, at school they all thought he was odd and different. He had supposed they were right, but didn't know exactly why. Now he had an answer! He wasn't like them, he was a spaceman! All he'd miss would be Timmy the dog, but Daddy had smiled and said they'd be able to visit him on Earth every Christmas – so they took him down to the local Pet Centre. And Andy admitted he had to laugh when Timmy was put in his vat and frozen – the expression on his face was priceless! Daddy smiled, of course, and even Mummy smiled a bit. There had been a lot of smiling that day.

Andy couldn't remember how long it had been since he'd seen Earth and Timmy. Since he'd become a spaceman! No, wait, he could work it out, if he tried hard. Six weeks. It was six weeks. And since they'd arrived there'd been the hunger and the rain and Uncle Bernard had been killed, of course, a lot of them had been killed. Andy thought he'd be able to cope with all of that, even Mummy's crying, if only Daddy would smile again. But Daddy didn't smile any more.

THE DAY THE DOCTOR ARRIVED AND CHANGED his life forever was also the day Andy had decided to envy the dog.

Whenever Andy asked about Timmy, his mother would say he wouldn't be *aware* he was living in a big ice cube. It would be as if he were asleep. But Andy, who had always been something of a light sleeper himself, found it hard to believe Timmy wouldn't have woken up by now. He would be bored, wouldn't he? Bored stiff, in fact!

But, all in all, bored wasn't such a very bad thing. Andy spent a fair bit of time being bored, hiding night and day in an underground bunker. But the boredom was accompanied by an awful lot of terror – so much, in fact, that he sometimes got confused as to whether he was meant to be bored or terrified at any particular moment and mixed the two up. He'd start shaking at the prospect of another hour of tedium, or yawning as his parents began screaming that this was it, this finally really *was* the end. Timmy didn't have all those complications to worry about.

It was a pretty momentous decision, the envying Timmy thing. And Andy chose to celebrate it by looking through the periscope. Mummy didn't like him to do it – she was frightened that what he'd see would be disturbing. But, let's face it, he'd already seen Uncle Bernard sliced up. Sliced up right in front of him! And that hadn't done him any harm, had it?

When Andy saw the two strangers trying to fend off the downpour, a part of him almost wanted to watch them die. Not in a cruel way – just to see whether it would be *different* this time. Or interesting. He guiltily supposed later that he hesitated for minutes before calling to his Mummy and Daddy, but it was barely seconds. The Doctor and Rose wouldn't have survived minutes.

'What are you doing? You'll let the rain in!'

'We can't leave them out there to die!' And his mother won, which was unusual. In almost all the arguments Mummy and Daddy had these days – and there were so, so many – she usually gave up.

As soon as the two strangers had clambered through the hatch, Daddy closed it with a bang. 'Thanks,' said the man. 'I think you just saved our lives.'

'Yes, we did,' muttered Daddy. He didn't sound too happy about it either.

'What's going on out there?' Andy liked the look of the girl immediately. She was frightened, of course – *everyone* on this planet was frightened. But she was angry too, she wanted answers. There was blood on her cheek; not deep, the rain must have just nicked it.

'Rose, you all right?'

'I'm fine.'

41

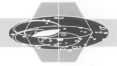

The man in the leather jacket nodded briefly, then seemed to lose interest. Andy wasn't so sure he liked him. He was looking around now, taking in the scene, assessing, judging. But his Daddy clearly didn't like him, and that was interesting. Yes, on balance, Andy reflected, he decided he would like this man after all. 'What's going on, Doctor?' asked the girl. Yes, Andy would like this *Doctor*.

'Bit of a heavy shower, what's all that about?' The Doctor was looking at his Daddy. Daddy looked away.

'You were lucky,' said Mummy. 'It's barely started yet.'

As if to prove her point, the tattoo beating on the metal roof got louder and more insistent. Banging at the hatchway, as if demanding to be let in.

ANDY'S PARENTS DIDN'T BOTHER TO TELL THE Doctor their names, and the Doctor didn't bother to ask. He was much more interested in looking out of the periscope as the rainstorm continued overhead. Andy introduced himself to Rose though.

'Hello, Andy,' she said. 'It's all right. Are you scared?'

And Andy began to tell her that he wasn't sure whether he was scared or bored any more, that whole problem he had distinguished between the two, and his consequent jealousy for his frozen dog. But he didn't get very far, because much to his surprise he burst into tears. Rose held him tight. His Daddy looked disgusted. Mummy looked away, a little embarrassed.

'I'm thirsty,' said Andy.

'There's hardly any water left,' his mother said. 'This has to last us. Are you sure you want it now?'

'I'm thirsty,' he said again.

The mother sighed, and poured some into a cup from a saucepan. Andy took it eagerly, took a sip. Then offered it to Rose.

'Not for her,' growled the father. Andy looked at his Mummy, but she didn't seem to want to argue any more. He mumbled a sorry to Rose, and passed the cup back.

'How long's this usually last?' asked the Doctor, still intent on the periscope.

'You shouldn't be in here,' said the man. 'We haven't food to share either.'

'Then we won't eat any...'

'You'll use up our air.'

'Yeah, well we'll hold our breath. You gonna answer my question or what?'

The woman spoke, a little nervously. 'The first time, it was just a few minutes. Caught us completely by surprise. But that was the worst. We lost twenty people, all the huts destroyed. After that, we all hid in the mines we'd been digging. But it's like the storm *knows*. It doesn't stop – won't stop – until it's got one or two of us.'

'So how long was the last storm?' asked Rose, still holding on to Andy.

'Nearly two weeks.'

The Doctor still sounded interested rather than alarmed. 'Odd how the rain doesn't fall evenly. Like it's coming down in funnels, all around.'

'It only rains on the roofs of the shelters,' said the man.

The Doctor, at last, looked away from the periscope. 'It's actually targeting you?'

'Oh yes,' said Andy glibly, and immediately looked surprised at how perfectly natural it sounded. 'It wants us dead.'

And no-one spoke for a while.

AT FIRST ROSE THOUGHT SHE WOULDN'T BE ABLE to stand the noise of the rainfall battering upon the steel above her head. But after about an hour she realised that the rhythm of it was changing – that there even *was* a rhythm. The water against the metal sounding more like notes, almost melodic. 'It's easing off,' she said. She spoke quietly, not wanting to disturb Andy, dozing with his head on her knees.

The woman laughed mirthlessly. 'It's trying to coax us out. You listen to it for too long, you almost believe it's talking to you. That it means you no harm.'

'That's what happened to Bill Anderson,' said her husband. 'Saw him do it. Just opened up the hatch, and stepped out into the rain.' His eyes were glassy, not looking at anybody, not looking at *anything*. 'And Bill wasn't even the sort who liked music. He had tattoos, for God's sake.'

If Rose closed her eyes, she could almost hear the rain beating out, '*Come and join us, come and join us, come and join us*'. And it sounded good, it sounded right. She looked at the Doctor. He hadn't spoken for ages, hadn't even wanted to look at these people. For a moment she flared with anger – why wasn't he helping, there must be something he could do, why couldn't he even say something? '*Come and join us, come and join us*', and why not? But the Doctor caught her eye. And shaking his head almost imperceptibly, took her hand.

The woman's voice was dull. 'It almost happened to me. One of the first nights after the rain started. After it *really* started, lasting for days and days. I was so frightened back then, I never thought I'd sleep again. But you get used to it, don't you? You get used to anything. The sound of the rain... it even seemed comforting after a while. Like a lullaby.'

The Doctor wasn't looking at the woman. When Rose did, he wouldn't let go of her hand.

'And it spoke to me. It said, Susie. It's all right, Susie... And no-one ever calls me Susie, not now, not since I was a kid... And I woke up. I just knew I had to get out of the shelter, into the rain, to feel it on my hands and my face. To feel refreshed...! I tried to be quiet, I didn't want to wake anybody, and I was so excited, you know? Like on Christmas morning, when you're in a hurry to open your presents. And the hatch was stuck, I couldn't open it well in the dark, but I didn't care, I had to open it, I pulled with all my strength, my wrist began hurting, I could hear the little bones popping, but it didn't matter, so long as I got outside. And the sound of the rain, urging me on, telling me it was going to be all right, it's all right, Susie...'

She fell silent. And for a while everyone thought the story was over. But then:

'I must have made more noise than I thought. And there you were. Standing behind me. Don't go, you said. Do you remember?'

'I remember,' said the man flatly.

'I asked you why not. Why shouldn't I go? You looked so frightened, so desperate, I felt quite sorry for you. Why not, I said. Because I love you, you replied. Do you remember?'

'Yes, I remember.'

'Because you loved me,' and the woman who wanted to be called Susie, but had never found anyone who would do so, smiled a little. 'Sometimes I wish you'd let me go.'

'Sometimes,' said the man, without bitterness, almost kindly, 'I wish I had too.'

'*Susie it's all right, Susie it's all right*', the rain seemed to be saying. And Rose realised she could no longer remember what she thought it had been saying to her. The Doctor was looking into her eyes, seemed relieved, and let her hand go.

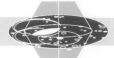

'SOMETHING'S HAPPENING,' SAID ANDY.

He was back at the periscope. It was the first thing he'd wanted when he'd woken up. He'd been embarrassed to find he'd slept against Rose, and had had an attack of acute shyness. Even though she was nice, and had talked to him now and then. He felt happier cradling the periscope for the while – you knew where you were with a periscope.

The Doctor hadn't talked to him at all. Somehow Andy wished he had. Now, for the first time, he took notice of what he said. They all did, as they gathered around the narrow viewer.

'It's concentrating on the Jackson shelter,' said Daddy. 'It must think it's nearly through.' And no more than fifty metres away, the rain was funnelling down upon the steel roof with what seemed like a whoop of joy.

And now there were two people emerging from the wrecked hatch. The man tried to run for it, but there was nowhere to run to; he was cut down by the streaming raindrops as if they were bullets fired from a million machine guns. The woman stood her ground, face up to the sky in surrender, for what was a few very long seconds.

Rose was shouting at the Doctor. 'We've got to help them!'

'There's nothing we can do,' he said.

Everyone looked on with sick fascination as the rain played over the fallen bodies, not yet realising they were dead, still trying to kill them. Rose realised no-one had given a thought to Andy, as hypnotised by it all as the rest of them, and led him away. For a moment Andy was furious, wanted to bite her. He'd miss it all! It was better than the boredom, wasn't it? Wasn't it?

'And now we're the last,' said the man. Rose turned to look at him, and was surprised to see he was pointing a pistol at the Doctor. He waved her over to join him.

'I want you to get out.'

'That isn't going to save you.'

'If it takes you. You and the girl. Maybe it'll leave us alone.'

'I know you're frightened,' said the Doctor. 'But you know that won't do you any good.'

'I just want to save my family!'

'We're not a family any more,' said the woman unexpectedly. And then: 'You're no husband to me, no father to Andy. You can't even keep a job.' And then: 'If we live through this, we're going to leave you. We're going to run away and not be with you any more. Because I can't stand it, Jack, I can't.'

For a moment the man stood still, as if he hadn't heard her. Then he slowly put the gun away. And sat in the corner without saying another word.

Now that the Jacksons were dealt with, the rain could afford to focus exclusively on the last remaining shelter. Rose would never have believed that steel could give way to rainfall alone, but as she saw it begin to buckle she realised it was only a matter of time.

'The rain's never going to stop, is it?' she asked the Doctor softly. 'What are we going to do?'

'Not yet,' he said.

After a while, Andy said, 'I'm thirsty.'

'There's no water left,' said his Mummy wearily. 'You drank it all, remember?'

'But I'm thirsty now.'

'Help me,' she said to the Doctor. She took a saucepan, and carefully unscrewed the hatch a fraction. As he held it steady, just ajar, she slid the pan outside. Immediately the rain sensed that there was new access to the shelter, and poured down all the more angrily. Odd drops spattered off the hatch edge, ricocheting on to the woman's hands, cutting out little flecks of skin. 'Now!' she cried at last, she pulled the pan inside, and the Doctor let the hatch bang back into place.

The water in the pan was seething, lapping against the sides, furious that it had been imprisoned. The woman slammed the lid down, and took the pan to a small stove. And as the water boiled inside, it *screamed*.

After the water had fallen silent, the heat was turned off, and the lid removed. The water seemed to Rose strangely still now that it was dead. It was poured into a cup, and passed around. Andy gulped at it greedily, the man silently took a sip.

'Not for us,' said the Doctor.

HIS DADDY FELL ASLEEP FIRST. HE'D SPENT THE evening disengaged from the rest of the group, so Andy only knew this because he heard the snoring. Then his Mummy curled up in the corner beside him for warmth, and pretty soon she was snoring too. Andy liked to look at his parents like that – they looked so perfect together when they were asleep.

Andy knew that the Doctor and Rose wanted him to sleep too. Rose kept on telling him how tired he must be, wouldn't he like to get some rest? And, in truth, he *was* tired. But he knew with absolute certainty that as soon as he wasn't awake to see them, Interesting Things would start to happen. So he faked it. A lifetime living with his parents, pretending that he couldn't hear their arguments, had made him good at that.

'I didn't want to involve them,' said the Doctor. 'Cos I don't think they're going to get out of this. I don't even know if *we* can.'

'You've hardly spoken to them. Even that poor little boy, and he *needs* some attention, Doctor!'

'And what d'you think I should say to him? Go on, what? I don't *want* to get to know him. What's the point?' Andy could hear how angry they both were, even though they were whispering, trying to make sure he wouldn't wake.

'The water's alive, isn't it?' said Rose. 'And they've been… drinking it…'

'Killing it. Yeah.'

'They weren't to know.'

'I don't think that's gonna make much difference. Do you?' Andy heard movement. 'Got to talk to it. If it can be talked to, got to try. Might be able to persuade them to let you go, Rose. You haven't done it any harm.'

'If you go out there, it's gonna kill you.'

'What else can I do?' Silence. Rose obviously had nothing to say to this. And then movement, as the Doctor went towards the hatch.

'Doctor,' she said, and Andy heard the Doctor pause. 'You've got to save them too. You've got to try. At least Andy. At least the boy.' Still that pause. More angrily, 'Well, *look* at him, at least!'

And Andy thought their eyes must now be on him. Rose, pleading. The Doctor, weighing him up. He felt the urge to laugh. He felt the urge to stand up, say, *ta-dah*, I wasn't asleep at all! He felt the urge to plead too. Please, save me. Please, you've got to try. He screwed his eyes ever tighter.

And then the hatch opened and the Doctor was gone. Andy couldn't pretend any longer.

'What's he going to do?' he cried.

'Andy!' Rose didn't know what to say.

'Is he going to try?' And Andy pushed himself beside her so he too could look through the periscope. Rose felt his little child excitement to see something exciting – even the Doctor's death – and for a moment she was revolted by it. And then she remembered he was a frightened little boy and forgave him.

The rain halted for a while, as if astonished by the Doctor's audacity. He stood still and opened his arms. Andy heard him shout out.

'*I want to talk!*'

And then, as one creature, the rain fell upon him. Every drop pouring down, hard, upon that lone man, still trying to talk, still trying to convince them. How could Andy have found this man impressive? He now looked so small and puny as he was beaten to the ground.

Rose scrabbled to the hatchway.

'No, Rose, don't!' cried Andy.

Rose shook him off.

'Stay with me! You be my Mummy. My Daddy, anything! Please…'

But she was through the hatch and running. Andy watched, sick with fear, as she sped towards the Doctor. Towards the rain – *let* the rain fall on her. And yet grasped hold of the Doctor, helping him to his feet. Stood with him. Held on to him.

And Andy saw the Doctor was *laughing*.

'YOU'VE GOT TO LEAVE RIGHT NOW.'

The Doctor and Rose stood before the dazed little family. They weren't even damp.

The father looked defeated and helpless. The mother was more defiant. She asked, 'And how do we know they'll let us get as far as the ship? How do we know they won't kill us anyway?'

The Doctor shrugged. 'You don't. But it's the best chance you've got. You're luckier than you should be.'

'I can't go back,' said the man. 'There's nothing for me on Earth. No job. No family.'

The woman said nothing.

'You have to hurry,' said Rose.

And Andy bent beside his father. He took his hand. 'It's all right, Daddy. You'll see.' And for a moment Rose almost thought she heard the coaxing rain within those words – *It'll be all right, Daddy, it'll be all right.*

His Daddy didn't say a word. But at least nodded. And at least stood up.

'Come on, Rose,' said the Doctor. He turned to leave without ever intending to look back.

'I wanted to be a spaceman,' said Andy. 'Can't I be a spaceman?'

The Doctor turned. And for the first time seemed to look at Andy properly.

'Not underground. Not hiding. A *proper* spaceman, seeing what's out there. There's more than you'd think, isn't there?'

And the Doctor smiled, and Andy basked in it. 'You be a spaceman,' he said. 'Just not here, and not today.'

Then he and Rose left.

The day that Andy became a spaceman was the day Daddy lost his job as a television set salesman. But, looking back, the day he *chose* to be a spaceman seemed to him more important. Living out in the stars. He led his parents back to their spaceship, and took them safely home. ●

DOCTOR · WHO
behind the scenes

WRITTEN BY **BENJAMIN COOK**

"You're going to have to throw yourselves around. Hang on to the console, flick the switches, pull down the levers. The more lurching, the better!"

So says James Hawes, a director of *Doctor Who*. He's talking the show's two lead actors through the complicated opening sequence for Episode 9, *The Empty Child*. Christopher Eccleston (the Doctor), wearing his usual leather jacket, and Billie Piper (Rose), sporting a Union Jack top, are frantically piloting the TARDIS, on the trail of a missile that's heading straight for the centre of London. James watches on a monitor as Chris and Billie rehearse – throwing themselves around the TARDIS, delivering their lines with such gusto, clinging desperately to the sloping-topped console as the central time rotor rises and falls.

"Maybe I should calm down a little," says Chris afterwards. "I don't want to break something!"

Ten minutes later, they're ready for a 'take'. Each shot usually has multiple 'takes' for a variety of reasons – an actor may miss a cue or forget a line, the director may want to try a slightly different angle, there may be a problem with lighting or sound. A look around the set reveals massive, continuous movement – there are lights going on, floor managers pointing at

cameras, technicians talking into head-sets, men fiddling with microphones. But when the bell rings to indicate that filming is about to start, the noise level on set quickly drops to zero.

TOP: Behind the scenes on *The Long Game*, with director Brian Grant (left), Simon Pegg as the Editor, and Billie Piper and Christopher Eccleston as Rose and the Doctor. The green screen above them will later be replaced by the CGI Jagrafess! **RIGHT:** Billie and Chris get to grips with the TARDIS on set for *The Empty Child*.

believable on set, chances are it'll look rubbish on screen. After the shoot, I sit with the editor and assemble all the shots in the cutting room. We refine the order, the timing and the look of the shots, to make sure that they tell the story as excitingly and grippingly as possible."

"For a take, then, please," says Dan Mumford, the first assistant director. "Nice and quiet everyone."

"And three, two, one… *action!*" calls out James.

On the first take, Chris tugs a little too hard on one of the levers on the console and it comes off in his hand! He says something rather upsetting, so the take is abandoned and the lever fixed. On the next take, Billie trips up on the grilled metal platform. Thankfully, the next take is perfect.

THE DIRECTOR

As well as having directed Episodes 9 and 10, set in London during World War Two, James will be overseeing further episodes in the next series. "As a director, I'm responsible for bringing

the scripts alive on the screen," he explains. "I'm involved in choosing the guest actors. I talk through the costumes, make-up and design of the sets with the art departments. Basically, I'm the one who needs to have an idea in my head of how everything will eventually look and sound."

On average, each 45-minute episode takes around twelve 11-hour days to film. That's about four minutes of screen time per day. The scenes for any given episode are shot out of order – the crew and featured cast moving from location to location, recording scenes from the shooting schedule until the entire script has been shot. "During the filming, I rehearse the actors and plan the shots with the camera team," says James. "It's up to me to decide whether we've got the shot right or whether we need another take. I also need to make sure that all the special effects are carefully planned and produced as convincingly as possible. If a monster doesn't look

THE TARDIS

A lot of the shooting for *Doctor Who* takes place in the hangars of an ordinary-looking industrial estate in Newport, South Wales. But on the inside, Unit Q2 is regularly transformed into space stations, elevator shafts, dark corridors... you name it. The TARDIS control room is the biggest and most impressive set housed here, and the show's designers are very proud of it. "The script for Episode 1 just described the inside of the TARDIS as a big wide room," explains

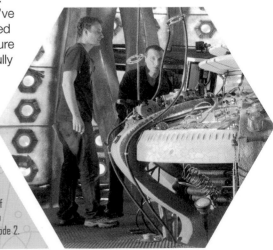

TOP: Director James Hawes takes Florence Hoath through a scene from The Empty Child LEFT: The scene gets underway – with a massive boom microphone so every line can be heard. ABOVE RIGHT: One of the actors takes a breather from his boiling Slitheen costume! RIGHT: Shooting on the TARDIS set for Episode 2.

48

Bryan Hitch, the concept designer, "so there was a feeling that it could be anything. It features in almost every story, so it needed to have a lasting impact. At the very first production meeting, I took along a doodle, which in essence is exactly want we built, but with modifications due to the size of the studio and the budget available. Walking onto the results of our labours was quite a wonderful moment."

Mark Gatiss, the writer of Episode 3 (*The Unquiet Dead*, set in Victorian Cardiff), was in studio on the day that the production team first saw the finished TARDIS control room.

"We all gawped when we walked onto the set," he remembers. "I love the coral idea and the bottom-of-a-pier feel of rust and decay. I think it's a long overdue stroke of genius to make the instruments on the console much less specific. It's much more patch-work and dangerous and thrown

together than I expected, but still with this amazing sense of awe and power. The perfect TARDIS!"

DALEKS AND MONSTERS!

Another big challenge for the design team was to update the look of the Daleks. "We knew that we had to appeal to a new audience," explains Bryan, "and with the scripts so fresh and vibrant, something a bit new was called for. The new Daleks stay true to the originals – the ones that first

TOP: Making *Dalek* underneath Cardiff's Millennium Stadium. Director Joe Ahearne stands far left, Dalek builder Mike Tucker on the far right. The rails help to keep the camera movements smooth. **ABOVE:** Another take for Billie! **LEFT:** The stars have their own special chairs! **RIGHT:** The amazing CGI extermination effect.

appeared in the 1960s – but they're chunkier and more robust, and the domed head and central sections spin round, which they didn't before."

Monsters are a staple ingredient of *Doctor Who*. "The marvellous thing is," says Russell T Davies, the head writer and executive producer of the show, "when this series was being planned, the Controllers of Drama at the BBC kept on asking us about monsters. 'Are there enough monsters?' they said. 'More monsters!' They wanted them just as much as I did! I thought we'd be sitting in meetings talking about budgets and schedules and viewing figures, but no – it was always monsters!"

As well as the dreaded Daleks, other creepy alien monsters include the Nestene Consciousness (which inhabits anything made of plastic, from shop window dummies to wheelie bins), the Moxx of Balhoon (a blue goblin-type creature in the Year Five Billion), and the Slitheen (a family of body-snatching aliens from the planet Raxacoricofallapatorius). But being a *Doctor Who* monster can be an uncomfortable experience. The actors have to stay in their monster costumes for hours at a time, which can be very hot, sweaty and tiring.

"The actors know that that it's not comfy," says James Bluett, who helped make many of the monster costumes, "but that's what they're getting paid for. And all respect to them – they put up with an absolute huge amount and keep their mouths shut, which I don't think I'd be able to." Does he ever read a script and think, nope, that's just too ambitious? "That's sometimes the first reaction, yeah," he laughs. "You put your head in your hands and close your eyes and you think, this *must* be possible to realise on screen… but how? But we work with an absolutely great team. Everyone supports one another, so everyone mucks in and we get it all done."

Some of the series' monsters – like Lady Cassandra (the oldest surviving

TOP: Jabe waits for her cue in Episode 2. **LEFT:** One of the scary new Daleks. Run away! **ABOVE:** The Moxx of Balhoon takes shape. **ABOVE RIGHT:** The amazingly detailed Big Ben model that was smashed up in Episode 4. **RIGHT:** The true face of a Slitheen!

human), the Gelth (ghostly beings from another dimension), and the Mighty Jagrafess of the Holy Hadrojassic Maxarodenfoe (which lives on Floor 500 of the Satellite Five space station) – are almost entirely computer-generated, the visual effects team adding them into existing footage. Episode 8, *Father's Day*, features computer-generated, gargoyle-like creatures called Reapers. "The visual effects guys are very proud of them," says Paul Cornell, the writer of that episode, "and rightly so. I love how the creatures move like real predators from the animal kingdom – that's something I mentioned a lot in the scripts. I hope kids are scared of them, 'cos that's what they're there for!"

Julie Gardner, the show's other executive producer, says: "I would like nothing better than viewers being genuinely scared by the monsters, but in a thrilling way – that they can laugh with their parents or their friends as they watch it. I hope we've been responsible in how we tell stories and what we've chosen to show. The scripts for the new series are just as inventive as they were in the old days."

THE GUEST ACTORS

The quality of the scripts has secured the programme some big name guest-star actors, including Simon Callow (Victorian writer Charles Dickens in *The Unquiet Dead*), Penelope Wilton (Harriet Jones, the kindly MP who helps the Doctor and Rose against the Slitheen), Simon Pegg (Satellite Five's sinister Editor, a servant of the Jagrafess), and Richard Wilson (Doctor

Constantine in London during the War). "I think these actors were surprised and delighted by the scripts they read," says Julie. "I don't think anyone knew what to expect. How were we going to bring back the show? But the writing across the series is incredibly strong. I know that Simon Callow, for instance, wanted to play Dickens because he knew so much about him – he's written books about Dickens – and he loved the way that Dickens had been written in that episode by Mark Gatiss. It's all in the writing."

Here's what Simon himself has to say: "I know from experience that most scripts that feature Dickens portray him as a colourful Victorian literary character and really don't understand him or his life. But it was obvious that Mark Gatiss' script was different. It was not only of the highest quality, but also the work of someone who really understood Dickens. It shows many facets of Dickens' character – in performance on stage, and tired and frail, because he was very ill at the time, but also his generous, kind-hearted nature. His encounter with the Doctor – they work together, and save the world – gives Dickens a new zest

GUEST STARS GALORE:
(Clockwise from top) Simon Callow as Charles Dickens (*The Unquiet Dead*), Simon Pegg as the Editor (*The Long Game*), Bruno Langley as Adam Mitchell (*The Long Game*), Richard Wilson as Doctor Constantine (*The Doctor Dances*), and Penelope Wilton as Harriet Jones (*World War Three*).

for life, which is a delightful idea. It's a very thoughtful script."

ON LOCATION

The Unquiet Dead was filmed partly on location. As well as building new sets, the production team often modify existing locations (the space station in the Year Five Billion, for example, was actually a Temple in Cardiff city centre), and so a street in nearby Swansea is doubling for Victorian Cardiff. The street has been closed and totally transformed for the shoot, with artificial snow, horse-drawn carriages, and lots of background artists (or 'extras') in period costume. It's 11 o'clock at night, and it's a lot colder out here than it is in Unit Q2. Chris and Billie rehearse with thick anoraks over their costumes, which they only remove when they go for a take. "Warm coats in," cries the first assistant director after each take, and someone runs back on with the anoraks.

Despite the cold, the actors are in high spirits. "Why do birds suddenly appear...?" sings Chris as he dances in the snow in his anorak to keep warm. At one point, he and Billie are so busy joking and dancing that they don't hear the director shout action, so he has to call it twice! The scene underway starts with the Doctor and Rose walking down the street, and then hearing a scream coming from inside the theatre...

"I love the Victorian period so much," says Mark Gatiss. "I love the language and the gloominess of the age, the wonderful Victorian love affair with death. I was on set for a little while, but I think I'll best remember sitting in the back of the theatre when the Gelth appear and the Doctor and Rose burst in – just sitting there, thrilled, with tears in my eyes, thinking 'Oh yes! It's my *Doctor Who*!'"

Back on set, Chris and Billie are hugging each other to keep warm. Some of the crew are huddled around the camera monitor, sniggering. The cameraman is cheekily drawing on the screen with a non-permanent marker pen, giving Billie a moustache and glasses. "You're not doing what I think you are, are you?" she asks.

"We'd never do that to you, Billie!" fibs the cameraman, and she laughs.

The next scene to be filmed tonight is relatively simple – and the closing one of the episode. Simon Callow is required to stride down the street, say a couple of lines, and walk off camera. Two machines pump fake snow into the air, while a group of extras sing a Christmas carol, and a horse-drawn carriage rattles down the street.

"This is amazing, really amazing," whispers Russell T Davies, who's on set tonight. "This is what I used to dream of as a kid: *Doctor Who* in the streets of Swansea!"

"And... action!" the director yells, and Simon as Dickens, looking triumphant, marches past the carriage and on through the snow. It's as magical, wintry a sight as you'll ever see.

But all in a night's work for the cast and crew of *Doctor Who*. ⬢

TOP LEFT: Charles Dickens saves Rose and the Doctor from the ghastly Gelth in *The Unquiet Dead*. **TOP RIGHT:** Filming the TARDIS arriving in 'London' (actually Cardiff!) for *Father's Day*. **ABOVE:** The awful Mrs Peace is brought (back) to life with clever make-up. **RIGHT:** The gaseous Gelth creatures were CGI creations.

What I Did On My Christmas Holidays
by SALLY SPARROW

MY NAME IS SALLY SPARROW.
I am 12 years old, I have auburn hair, braces you can hardly see, a dent in my left knee from where I fell off a bicycle when I was ten, and parents. I also have a little brother called Tim. My Mum told Mrs Medford that Tim Wasn't Planned, and you can tell because his nose isn't straight and his hair sticks up and I can't believe you'd do all that on purpose. Or his ears.

I am top in English, and Miss Telfer says I have an excellent vocabulary. I have sixteen friends who are mainly girls. I haven't taken much interest in boys yet, because of the noise.

This is the story of the mysterious events that happened to me at my fat Aunt's cottage at Christmas and what I discovered under the wallpaper of my bedroom, which caused me to raise my eyebrows with perplexity.

I was staying at my fat Aunt's cottage because my Mum and Dad had gone on a weekend away. Tim was staying with his friend Rupert (who I don't think was planned either because of his teeth) and I found myself once more in the spare bedroom at my Aunt's cottage in the countryside, which is in Devon.

I love my Aunt's cottage. From her kitchen window you can only see fields, all the way to the horizon, and it's so quiet you can hear water dripping off a leaf from right at the end of the garden. Sometimes, when I lie in bed, I can hear a train far away in the distance and it always fills me with a big sighing feeling, like sadness, only nice. It's good, my bedroom at my aunt's. Really big, with a wardrobe that rattles its hangers when you walk past it and huge yellow flowers on the wallpaper. When I was little I used to sit and stare at those flowers and when no one was looking I'd try to pick them, like they were real flowers. You can still see a little torn bit where I tried to peel one off the wall when I was three, and every time I go into the room, the first thing I do is go straight to that flower and touch it, just remembering and such. I've talked about it with my Dad and we think it might be Nostalgia.

It's because of that flower and the Nostalgia that I first met the Doctor.

WRITTEN BY
STEVEN MOFFAT

ILLUSTRATIONS BY
MARTIN GERAGHTY

IT WAS THREE DAYS BEFORE CHRISTMAS. I'D JUST arrived at my fat Aunt's house, and as usual, I'd hugged her and run straight upstairs to my room, to hang all my clothes in the rattley wardrobe. And as usual I'd gone straight to the torn yellow flower on the wall, and knelt beside it (I'm bigger now) and touched it. But this time, I did something different. I don't know why. I heard my Aunt calling from downstairs that I shouldn't be too long, because she'd cooked my favourite and it was on the table, and usually I'd have run straight down. Maybe it was because I knew she'd want to talk about school and sometimes you don't want to talk about school (sorry, Miss Telfer) especially if you've got braces and frizzy hair and people can be a bit silly about that kind of thing, even if they're supposed to be your friends. Maybe it was because I was thinking about being three, and how much smaller the flowers looked now. Actually I think it was because Mary Phillips had made up a song about my hair and I was feeling a bit cross and my eyes were all stingy and blurry the way they get when you know you're going to cry if you don't really concentrate. Anyway, my fingers were resting right on the torn bit, and I was thinking about the song, and frizziness and such, and suddenly it was like I just didn't care! And I started to tear the paper a little bit more! Just a tiny bit at first, I just sort of tugged it to see what would happen. And I kept going! And you know sometimes it's like you're

in a dream – you're doing something, but it doesn't feel like you're *doing* it, more like you're just watching? Well, I went right on and peeled the whole flower off the wall. A whole streak of wallpaper and I just ripped it right off!

And then, oh my goodness me! I just stared!

I once read in a story about a girl who got a fright and the writer said she felt her hair stand on end. I thought that was rubbish and would look really stupid, like my brother. I thought the writer was probably making that bit up, because it couldn't happen. But I was wrong. I could feel it happening now, starting up my neck, all cold, then all my scalp just fizzing and tingling.

And here is what was written under the wallpaper. 'Help me, Sally Sparrow'.

I looked closer, trying to work out if it was a trick, and noticed something else. More words, written just under those ones, but still covered by the wallpaper. Well, I thought, I'd already ruined it so I had nothing to lose. As carefully as I could, I tore off another strip. Beneath the words was just a date. 24/12/85.

Twenty years ago, someone in this room, asked for my help. Eight years before I was even born!

'CHRISTMAS EVE, 1985? SORRY LOVE, I DON'T really remember.' My Aunt was frowning at me across the dinner table, trying to think.

'Can you really try, please? It's ever so important. Maybe you had guests, or friends staying or something? Maybe in my room.'

'Well we always had Christmas parties, when your uncle was still alive.'

'He *is* still alive, he's living in Stoke with Neville.'

'You could check in the shed.'

'Why would he be in the shed, Auntie, he's very happy with –'

'For the *photographs*.' She was looking at me, all severe now. 'If we had a party we always had photographs. I always keep photographs, I'll have a look around.'

'Thanks, Auntie!'

'What does it matter though? Why so interested?'

I nearly told her, but I knew she'd laugh. Because really, if you think about it, there was only one explanation. Coincidence. There must have been another Sally in the family I'd never heard about, and whoever had written that on the wall twenty years ago, they hadn't meant *me*, they'd meant *her*. They'd meant that mysterious other Sally from twenty years ago. I wondered what she was like. I wondered

where she was now, and if her hair was frizzy. And I wondered most of all why she'd been kept a dark secret all these many years. Perhaps she'd been horribly murdered for Deadly Reasons!

As I was about to go to bed, I looked hard at my Aunt – the way I do when I'm warning adults not to lie to me – and asked, 'There was another Sally Sparrow, wasn't there, Auntie? I'm not the first, am I?'

My Aunt looked at me really oddly for a moment. I half expected her to stagger back against the mantelpiece, all pale and clutching at her bosom, and ask in quivery tones how I had uncovered the family secret and have terrible rending sobs. But no, she just laughed and said 'No, of

course not! One Sally Sparrow is quite enough. Now off to bed with you!'

I lay in my bed but I couldn't sleep! There had to be another Sally, there just *had* to be. Otherwise someone from twenty years ago was trying to talk to me from under the wallpaper and that was just stupid!

When my Aunt came in to kiss me goodnight (I always pretend to be asleep but I never am) I heard her put something on my bedside table. As soon as I heard her bedroom door close, I jumped and switched the light on! Maybe this was it! Maybe this was her dark confession – the truth about the other Sally Sparrow, and her Dreadful Fate. Sitting on my bedside table was a box. I gasped horrendously! I wondered how big a box would have to be to contain human remains! I narrowed my eyes shrewdly (and also bravely) and looked at the label on the lid (though I did think labelling murdered human remains would be a bit of an obvious mistake).

The label said 'Photographs 1985'.

The Christmas party ones were right at the bottom, and took me ages to find. They were just the usual kind, lots of people grinning and drinking, and wearing paper hats. My fat Aunt was there, still with Uncle Hugh, and my Mum and Dad too looking all shiny and thin. And then I saw it! My eyebrows raised in perplexity again, slightly higher this time. Because standing right in the middle of one of the photographs was a man with a leather jacket and enormous ears. He was in the middle of a line of grown-ups laughing and dancing, but he was looking right at the camera and holding up a piece of paper like a sign. And on the sign it said 'Help me, Sally Sparrow!'

I gasped in even more amazement. There *was* another

Sally Sparrow and obviously she was taking the photograph. And probably she was a bit deaf, and you had to talk to her with paper signs, because hearing aids hadn't been invented yet.

And then I looked at the next photograph. And that's when everything changed. Suddenly it was like the school bell was ringing in my ears and I could feel my heart thudding in my chest so hard you could probably have seen the buttons bouncing on my pyjamas.

There was the man again, at the back of the photograph, holding up another piece of paper. And this one said 'Look under the wallpaper again.'

As I reached for the wallpaper again my hand was shaking away like when you try to do your homework on the school bus. The next bit of writing was much longer and this is what it said. 'This isn't a dream, and by the way you should never try to do your homework on the school bus. I'm going to prove this is real. Think of a number, any number at all, and then get dressed, find a torch, and see what's carved in the bark of the furthest tree in the garden.'

When people think of a number, they always think of ten, or seven or something. They never think of a really big, stupid one. So I did, I thought of a big, stupid one. Then I halved it. Then I added my age. Then I took away Tim's age. Then I added four, just because I felt like it. And then a few minutes later, I was standing in the garden, shivering, staring at the furthest tree.

And there it was, carved like it had been there forever. No one ever thinks of the number 73. Except me. And the man who had carved the furthest tree in my Aunt's garden twenty years ago.

I sat on my bed for ages, just shaking and wondering what to do now. But it was obvious really. I tore off the next strip of wallpaper. This time, it just said 'Top shelf in the living room, right at the back.'

The top shelf was where my Aunt kept all

her videos. She hardly ever watched television, never mind videos, so they were all very dusty. And right at the back, jammed half way down the gap at the back of the shelf, was a tape that looked like it had been there for a long time. And stuck on it, a post-it. It said 'FAO Sally Sparrow'.

I slipped it into the VCR and kept the television volume really low, so as not to wake my Aunt.

And there, grinning like a loon from the television, was the man from the photographs. 'Hello, Sally Sparrow! Any questions?'

He was sitting in my bedroom! Only the walls were bare, and there was a pair of ladders in the middle of the room, like someone was decorating. I could hear party music coming from somewhere downstairs, and I wondered if it was the party in 1985.

'Well, come on, Sally!' the man was saying, 'You've gotta have questions. *I* would.'

I frowned. Not a lot of point in asking questions when the man you're asking can't hear them!

'Who says I can't hear you?' grinned the man.

I stared! I think I probably gasped. My eyebrows were practically bursting out of the top of my head. It was ridiculous, it was *impossible*. I hadn't even said that *out loud*.

'No, you didn't,' said the man, checking on a piece of paper, 'You just thought that.' He glanced at the paper again. 'Oh, and yeah, you did gasp.'

'Who are you?' I blurted.

'That's more like it, now we're cooking. I'm the Doctor. I'm a time traveller and I'm stuck in 1985, and I need your help.'

I had so many questions racing round my head I didn't know which one to pick.

'How did you get stuck?' I said.

'Parked my time machine in your Aunt's shed. Was

just locking up, and it... well... *burped*.'

'Burped??'

'Yeah, burped. Shot forward twenty years, I hate it when that happens.'

I looked out the window to where my Aunt's shed stood at the end of the garden. And I noticed there was something glowing at the windows. Suddenly, I was just a little bit afraid. 'So it's *here* then?'

'Exactly. Nip out to your Aunt's shed, you'll find a big blue box, key still in the door. Could just stick around for twenty years and pick it up myself but I don't want it falling into the wrong hands.' He leaned forward to the camera, and his eyes just *burned* at me. 'And I know *you're* not the wrong hands, Sally Sparrow. So I want you to fly it back to me!'

I swallowed hard. This was totally freaky.

He glanced at his paper again. 'You've got another question, I think.'

He was right. 'You're just on video tape. How can you *hear* me??'

He smiled. 'Actually, I can't. Can't hear a thing. I just happen to know everything you and me are gonna say in this whole conversation.'

'How??'

'Cos Mary Phillips made up a song about your hair.'

I could hardly breathe for all the gasping.

'And you punched her, didn't you, Sally Sparrow? And then you got a punishment?'

My face was burning. How did he know all this? I hadn't even told my Mum and Dad.

'You got Christmas homework. An essay about what you did over the Christmas holidays.' He grinned. 'And I've got a copy!'

And this is freakiest part of all. Because he held a copy of the actual essay I'm writing right now!!

'I know everything you're gonna ask when you see this tape, cos I've read the essay you wrote about it. That's how I knew what to write on the wall – you'll have to show me exactly where, by the way – and that's how I knew what number you were thinking of.'

'But… but…' I could hardly think for my mind racing. 'How did you get a copy of my Christmas homework! I haven't even written it yet!!'

'Told you, I'm a time traveller. I got it in the future. From a beautiful woman on a balcony in Istanbul.' He smiled, like it was happy memory. 'She was some sort of spy, I think. Amazing woman! I'd just had a sword fight on the roof with two Sontarans, and she saved me from the second one. Then she gave me your Christmas homework and told me to keep it on me at all times, cos I'd need it one day.' He grinned. 'She was right!'

A spy, in the future, was going to have a copy of my Christmas homework? Talk about pressure!

He was looking at his watch. 'Okay, that's just about time up. Gonna need you to go to the time machine, and fly it here.'

'I can't fly a time machine. I had stabilisers on my bike till I was *nine*!!'

'Sally, I absolutely know that you can do this. And do you know how?'

'How?'

'Because I've read to the end of the story.' He laughed. 'Also – you hear that noise?'

Coming from the television, a terrible wheezing and groaning.

'What's that??'

He was still grinning. 'That's you!'

Behind the man, a huge blue box just appeared out of thin air. I stared at it. There were words over the door and I squinted closer to read them.

I should've known. He looked like a policeman!

'That's your time machine?'

'Yep. Like it?'

'But who flew it there?'

You could almost get tired of that grin. 'You did!'

The doors on the big blue box were opening. And then the most amazing thing ever. *I stepped out of the box!!* Me! Sally Sparrow! Another me stepped out of the time machine and waved at the camera.

'Hello, Sally Sparrow, two hours ago!' said the other me. 'It's great in there, you're going to love it. It's bigger on the inside!'

'See?' said the man. 'Told you you could fly a time machine.'

'Yeah, it's easy!' said the other Sally, 'It homes in on his watch, anyway. You just have to press the reset button next to the phone.'

'Who told you that?' I asked her.

A frown clouded her face. 'I did,' she said, and looked puzzled.

The man looked a little cross about that. 'Yeah, well before you set off any more time paradoxes... Sally Sparrow!' he gave me a Teacher look from the television. 'Go and do your homework!'

'Yeah!' said the other Sally, 'You've got to write the essay before you can fly the time machine. It'll take you about two hours.'

'That's enough, both of you!' said the man, 'Got enough paradoxes going on here, without you pair having a chat!'

'But, listen, it's going to be *great*!' said the other Sally. And she gave me the biggest, most excited smile ever.

And oh goodness! You *can* see my braces!

AND SO HERE I AM, FINISHING MY essay. It's nearly two o'clock in the morning, and in a minute I'll be fetching the shed key from the kitchen drawer and setting off across the garden on the trip of a lifetime. A big, amazing adventure. And not my last one either, oh no! Just the first of lots and lots, for the rest of my life probably. Suddenly I don't care what my Aunt is going to say about the torn wallpaper or what Mary Phillips thinks about my hair. I'll go back to school after the holidays and just be nice to her, and she can make up all the songs she wants. I'll join in, if it makes her happy.

You see, I know the best thing in the world. I know what's coming. I asked the man one more question before the end of the tape. I asked how a beautiful woman spy in the future could have a copy of my Christmas homework.

'Can't you guess?' he smiled. Not grinned, smiled. 'Her name,' he continued, 'Was Sally Sparrow.'

The big blue box is waiting in the shed at the end of the garden. And I've finished my homework. ●

WRITTEN BY **GARETH ROBERTS**

Inside the
TARDIS

FROM THE OUTSIDE, THE TARDIS just looks like a battered blue wooden box. Your grandparents would recognise it as a police telephone box – they might have used one to call for help in the days before mobile phones. But the box is only a disguise. Take a step inside and it's another world; a massive alien ship with the power to travel anywhere in space and time, property of the Doctor – his unique mode of transport, product of the lost wisdom of the Time Lords and, since the destruction of his planet, the only home he knows.

The word TARDIS is made up from the initials **T**ime **A**nd **R**elative **D**imension **I**n **S**pace. The Doctor's race, the Time Lords of Gallifrey, possessed the most advanced technology in the universe, and built TARDISes to explore. Centuries ago the Doctor stole his TARDIS and fled Gallifrey, for reasons he's never made clear, and became an exile in time and space. On a visit to London in 1963, the chameleon circuit – which is supposed to change the TARDIS's exterior shape so it blends in with its

POLICE PUBLIC CALL BOX

POLICE TELEPHONE
FREE
FOR USE OF
PUBLIC

ADVICE & ASSISTANCE
OBTAINABLE IMMEDIATELY

OFFICER & CARS
RESPOND TO ALL CALLS

PULL TO OPEN

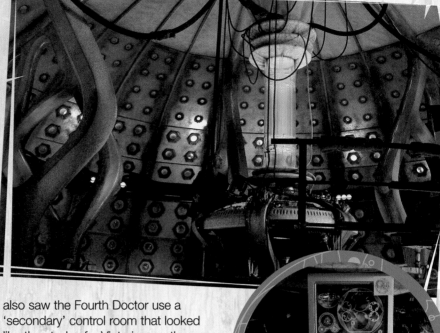

surroundings wherever it lands – broke down, so it's been trapped in the shape of a police box ever since.

And the chameleon circuit isn't the only thing in the TARDIS that doesn't work. It's a very old ship after all, and the Doctor isn't much of a pilot – when all else fails he's been known to bash at the controls with a hammer! His navigation's a bit hit and miss – he got Rose to Platform One to see the end of the world with no trouble at all, but miscalculated the return journey to her estate by a whole year.

A DANGEROUS POWER

The six-sided control console is the heart of the TARDIS, from which the Doctor operates its ancient engines. The central column rises and falls during journeys through the space-time vortex and comes to a halt at landing – or, as the Doctor calls it, materialisation. There's also a scanner screen which shows the immediate surroundings, using a camera fitted into the light on the police box roof. The Doctor even leaves himself post-it notes on the console, written in bizarre alien hieroglyphics. A power the Doctor refers to as 'a gift of the TARDIS' enables him and Rose to understand whatever language is spoken anywhere they land. And concealed within the console is the TARDIS's power source – a frighteningly powerful energy that has the power to warp time itself, as one of the wicked Slitheen discovered when it threw her back in time to when she was merely an alien egg. Rose had to unleash this dangerous power herself when she got separated from the Doctor during their battle with the Daleks, with devastating results…

Nowadays the Doctor likes the TARDIS control room big and organic, but in the past he experimented with a variety of different designs; using the ship's architectural configuration system he was able to swap bits of the interior about as if it was a computer program. For many years, the earlier Doctors used a control room with the same basic layout; gleaming white, with glowing circular designs on the walls and bric-a-brac from previous adventures scattered about. But we

also saw the Fourth Doctor use a 'secondary' control room that looked like the study of a Victorian gentleman, and the Eighth Doctor made it huge and gothic, like the inside of a ruined cathedral – complete with bats!

VIRTUALLY INDESTRUCTIBLE

The TARDIS isn't just the control room either. Rose has made use of the ship's well-stocked wardrobe, packed with clothes from just about anywhere in the universe, and there are miles of corridors and rooms beyond the main section. In earlier adventures we saw a huge swimming pool, a greenhouse, an art gallery, a hospital, a cricket pavilion, and the Cloisters; an ivy-covered courtyard that the Doctor liked to pace around when thinking. There are also many bedrooms for use by his companions, and a food machine which you can use to dial up any snack you fancy.

In theory, the TARDIS is indestructible – it's survived falls from clifftops, being pushed down a mine by angry Luddites, and, as the Doctor told Rose, an assault by the assembled hordes of Genghis Khan! Keys to the TARDIS look like very ordinary doorkeys, but they're more than that; when the TARDIS is about to materialise the key glows, and the Doctor was able to use his key as a link to the TARDIS when time was disrupted by Rose's interference with her own father's history.

The TARDIS is a very big part of the Doctor's life – without it, he'd be stuck on one planet in one time zone, like any other person. It's changed Rose's life too. And when you hear the groaning of those ancient engines, a light flashes, and a battered blue wooden box appears out of nowhere, you know it's time for them to begin another adventure, somewhere – anywhere – in space and time… ●

TOP: The Doctor at the controls of the TARDIS – and a close look at the scanner screen, covered in post-it notes!
ABOVE: The Eighth Doctor's rather gothic TARDIS – complete with bats!
LEFT: The TARDIS as it first appeared during the 1960s.

PUZZLE SOLUTIONS

ROBOT ROSE

The ten mix-ups were:

The **Nestene Consciousness** brought plastic to life, not the Slitheen; Rose's boyfriend is **Mickey**, not Mike; the end of the world was in the year **five billion**, not two billion; Rose and the Doctor met Charles Dickens in **Cardiff**, not Edinburgh; it was the **Slitheen**, not the Nestenes, who tried to blow up the world, and they were disguised as **politicians** not journalists; the Dalek adventure happened in **America**, not Canada; the Dalek killed **itself**, the Doctor didn't kill it; the space station was called **Satellite 5**, not Satellite 9; and the villain there was the **Jagrafess**, not Cassandra.'

TARDIS TEASER

The number of unarmed Dalek ships was: Three.

THE VAN STATTEN CODE

The message reads: BEWARE THE BAD WOLF.

UNIT INITIATION TEST

The solutions are:

• There are 16 letters in the phrase 'The Dalek Alphabet'!
• If you remembered to say that the bath must be emptied first, then 20 minutes. If you didn't, then it will take no time at all as the bath is already full!
• No Daleks!
• Any of the following is an acceptable answer: 'Yes', 'No', 'I,T'!

LOST LUGGAGE

• Dark blue.
• Police Public Call Box.
• Both doors have handles – one on the box itself, one on the telephone panel.
• The door on the right has the lock.
• Inwards.
• Six.
• Time And Relative Dimension In Space ('Dimensions' is also acceptable).

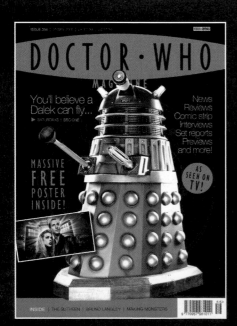